Spiral Out

SPIRAL OUT
Copyright © 2013 u.v. ray
All rights reserved
ISBN: 978-1-291-52231-0

Spiral Out is presented as works of fiction and any likeness to any person living or dead is entirely coincidental.

10 9 8 7 6 5 4 3 2 1
First Printing

Cover and Interior Art © 2013 Steve Hussy

No part of this book may be used or reproduced in any manner whatsoever without written permission from the publisher, except in the case of quotations embodied in critical articles and reviews.

For all queries contact:
Murder Slim Press, 29 Alpha Road, Gorleston, Norfolk.
NR31 0LQ   United Kingdom

Murder Slim Press are:
Steve Hussy and Richard White

Published by Murder Slim Press 2013
www.murderslim.com

Printed and bound in the UK by the MPG Books Group,
Bodmin and King's Lynn

Spiral Out

Introduction
by Jeffrey Frye

Simply put, u.v.ray is one of the great underground writers in international publication today. One of the great unknowns. Many writers bill themselves as "underground writers" because they think it's avant garde or literally advantageous to do so, but u.v.ray has earned this designation. He is truly an outsider, yet he's also a member of a club for which he has no desire to belong; a club that includes greats such as Bukowski, Fante, and Salinger. His writing is passionate and sometimes philosophically blunt with impetus that seems to be pulled from the acerbic ether and has a unique style that is unparalleled. A unique style that I've come to refer to as "Ucerbic."

I was first exposed to u.v.ray while on a writer's retreat in a gated community in the mountains of Central Pennsylvania. My sister ordered and sent me his critically acclaimed chapbook WE ARE GLASS and I spent a long, dark, winter night going into the world that is u.v.ray. Like all truly great writing, his stories provoked emotions within me, and they made me not only identify with his prose, but also feel it. Some of his stories made me smile and laugh (even when he sometimes wasn't trying to), and some of them made

Spiral Out

me angry. But more than anything, his writing made me want to read more. Like all great writing does.

What you now hold in your hands and are about to experience is the voice of a wounded and beautiful soul. A relevant voice of one of the great unknowns, and a voice that's a part of every single person who's honest enough to admit it. So sit back and hang on and enjoy the ride...and get ready to Spiral Out.

Jeffrey Patrick Frye
Bruceton Mills, West Virginia

Spiral Out

1

I have no real idea what happened that afternoon, everything is a blur. All I know is I'm in a panic, on the phone in the call box at the top of Lysways Street to my father, telling him I'm in a little situation here and I need to speak to Offenbach. I tell him, get Offenbach to call me now at this call box, I'll be waiting. I need to ask him how to get rid of a freshly dead body.

2

The view from the apartment was cold and bleak. I could see the city spread out before me. The sun hadn't yet come up and the sprawling mass of city lights glittered like a swarm of fireflies in the blackness. Already I hankered for whisky but I'd already drank myself dry.

On Sundays I usually started at about eleven in the morning. I'd drink two bottles of wine and smoke about eight or nine joints before I went out, so I was already pretty bombed by the time I got down the boozer for the rest of the day and night. I'd go down and wouldn't stop drinking until they stopped serving. If I managed to pull some bird I'd drag her back to the flat and drink until I was unconscious. I'd wake up in the morning and the birds had usually gone. And that was just my Sunday wind-down after a speed fuelled Saturday night.

I'm not entirely sure what she saw in me but in Lydia's case, when I woke up in the morning she was amazingly one of the few who were still there. And that was the beginning of our relationship. It was light outside and the diffused sunlight through the bedroom curtains bathed Lydia's naked body in a magnificent golden hue. She was up, already showered and I watched her fiddling in her overnight stay bag; fixing herself up to leave for her modelling job in London. I dressed and made coffee. We sat at the kitchen table talking as we drank it. As she held the steaming cup between her hands her diamond encrusted rings glinted in the light from the window.

With her long black hair and that petite little body she looked better every time I looked at her. Face pretty and flawless as a china-doll, white and perfect in the disco-lights. Her shirt was open right down between her firm looking little breasts, revealing a hint of front-fastening red lace bra. But you don't tell the most beautiful women they are so. They hear that

Spiral Out

a dozen times a day from all the other grovelling dickheads. So I was straight with her from the start; I told her right then and there in the club that ordinarily men of my calibre are not attracted to women like her and all I wanted to do was take her home and grab her by the neck and throw her violently on the bed. So she laughs a little bit drunk and shrugs and says: okay then, take her home and rape her. Rape me. Fuck me as hard as you like, she said. Fuck me like you're raping me, do what you like to me.

I yanked her jeans off and ripped her little red knickers off. Oh that shaved pussy. Rose red swollen labia. I pinned her arms down above her head and she breathed in my ear: *fucking rape me.*

I devoured her tongue, the peppery red lipstick. I wrapped my hands in her long hair and pulled her head back hard and fucked it all right out of my system. We both collapsed, gasping, tearing at each other so brutally we punctured each other's skin with our fingernails and I came inside her in a swirling fusion of pleasure and pain. We lay there breathless, as if in the aftermath of a hurricane; devastated, unable to speak. My heart was beating so hard I thought it was going to give out.

These were the first physical sensations I'd had in I didn't know how long, like a sleeping snake that had been coiled inside me, and just for those brief moments I saw everything I'd ever thought beautiful in the world was right there in my arms in the fleshly form of Lydia. My heart felt like a tiny bird held in the cool palms of her porcelain hands.

She finished her morning coffee, kissed me on the mouth, and then slung her Louis Vuitton bag over her shoulder and briskly walked out the door with her glossy black hair flowing behind her. I didn't notice the hefty clunk as the door slammed shut so much as the tender residue of lipstick left on the coffee cup, compounded by the resounding waves of quietness that invaded the whole apartment in her wake. I was alone again. And nothing seemed to fill my sense of emptiness.

A few days later she went to Terracina in Italy on some modelling job. But surprisingly she sent me her telephone number scrawled in red lipstick surrounded by a mascara black heart on the back of a photograph in which she was looking absolutely tantalising in a short blue and white polka-dot summer dress. I should never have called that number. The symbolism was there, even before I became aware of the reality of it like some blazing warning. I wouldn't call myself superstitious, I didn't believe in fairies. But purely by analytical observation I had to say that when Lydia was around I didn't have any luck at all. She brought along with her only badness.

Lydia fucked everything up. Her own life, I mean. She was a fuck-up and all she ever did was fuck everything up; for herself and anyone who became embroiled in her crap, like a

Spiral Out

vortex dragging everything in. A femme fatale that floats into your life gentle as a butterfly. She was a model who worked in London and I have no idea why the most beautiful ones amongst womenfolk are also the most fucked-up in the head. But she was beautiful in the same way a bird of prey is beautiful, or a lion. Beautiful but deadly. And she became like a stab wound to the gut, leaking stomach-acid into my bloodstream, poisoning me slowly.

In truth, I'd lost all interest in a woman's conversation, whatever was going on in her mind. The rudiments of the female species held no fascination for me and when they spoke I may have nodded and pretended to be listening whilst I watched their lips and thought only of whether or not I wanted to stick my cock in her mouth. With my increasing feelings of isolation, women could sense that I did not believe in love and they were nothing more than objects to me. I didn't need no beautiful face with a characterful little scar or slight blushing of her cheeks when she laughs. I wanted my women expressionless; as plastic looking as possible with heavily made-up faces and glassy, doll-like eyes and doll-like bodies. Something to be possessed.

I have found more beauty in my possessions, the antiques I have collected than I have in people. Such possessions last longer than people, last longer than love. Men hate women and that's a fact. They might not admit it but all

Spiral Out

men hate women. They hate the sexual power women wield over them and how weak and helpless it makes them feel. And it's all part of a strange dynamic I've observed. I often wondered why so many women seemed to like being mistreated, why they are so frequently attracted to men who make no attempt to hide their misogyny, men who do not refrain, like most other men, from calling a woman a cunt when she is clearly behaving like one.

Most men hate the fact that women don't get treated as equals when they deserve to be. No one refrains from calling a man a cunt. Women usually escape such judgements purely because men grow up in subjugation to the mother. Call a woman a cunt, as you'd call a man a cunt, and these militant feminists soon get up on their high-horse. But a man that unashamedly calls a woman a cunt seems to command some kind of unspeakable respect amongst women. I am speaking both literally and metaphorically, of course, about such men's overall attitude towards women. The sticking point for most men is the pandering to the mother. Those that treat women as equals, rather than surrendering themselves to the mother figure like little sissies, are far more likely to call a woman a cunt.

And what does it matter? No one truly loves anyone else just for who they are. In the end we simply choose to acquaint ourselves with people who make us feel better in some

Spiral Out

way, someone who fills a void within us. We are all trapped inside the shell of ourselves. That's how it is, and I don't care if anyone else disagrees with me because that simply indicates that they are wrong and I am right. It's all about voids. Voids in the universe. Voids within ourselves.

3

Watching the liquid in the barrel of a junkgun being pumped into your arm while you're already half gone, slumped in the armchair is like returning to the womb. It all seems so natural. It all comes to you in an epiphany, as if time itself dissolves and you're asking yourself the question: is this how it ends? Disjointed memories of your life sweep across your drooping eye-lids and yet you can't even remember your own name. I was a fearless overdoser; give me a handful of pills and I'd swallow the lot without even asking what they were. Like a fucking Zen priest or whatever they're called, I set out with one mantra: Obliterate Consciousness. Obliterate Consciousness. Obliterate Consciousness.

Quite often, when I look at photographs, I'm distracted by something in the background; a beautiful face in the crowd, perhaps, or someone staring blankly out the window of an idling bus. I become enthralled. I look for the more unnoticed aspects of life. They seem more meaningful to me. But what can I say? I've always been something of an escapist. I've always preferred images to reality. Images that have no deeper meaning, other than the surface upon which you can impress your own thoughts. It's just better that way. People have always let me down. It's just the nature of how everyone has their own trajectory in life. It's all near misses, near encounters. We are like crossing comet tails. But in the end no one is to blame, we are all solitary travellers at the mercy of gravitational influences pulling us this way or that.

No one truly loves anyone else just for who they are. They just hide behind false manners and smiles. In the end we simply choose to acquaint ourselves with people who make us feel better in some way, someone who fills a void within us. Well, in truth, I don't know if I can state unequivocally that love does not exist, I can only state that it is outside my own personal experience. It's like the sound of distant traffic. Some of us are outcasts all our lives. You get on a bus and as if by instinct almost everyone puts their bag on the empty seat next to them. You see the implicit hatred in their eyes. You are a black sheep left alone to be torn apart by wolves.

With your eye-lids turning blue in some cheap hotel there's nothing to worry about any more. In the end everything is silent and beautiful. Just pull the trigger and in an unknowable instant blow your brains across the ceiling. And

Spiral Out

when they eventually find you the only thing left is for some poor bastard to come and scrape your oblivious half-decomposed carcass up off the floor. While somewhere across town in the bowels of the hospital new life is spat from the infected womb of its mother. And as the infant draws its first choking breath of air you can hear its scream of protest ring out all over this shattered city.

Sometimes I want to go outside and scream into the night just to hear the echo come back to me and prove in some way that I am really here. There's no beauty in life any more, no joy. I only ever wanted to shut myself away in a fortress of my own making, to erect impenetrable walls all around me. With these solitary thoughts I was just trying to preserve something before my mind was finally and completely shot to hell.

4

It was a dirty, black skied morning. An amphetamine induced insomniac unable to sleep properly again, on weekdays I could quite accurately guess the time by lying in the dark counting the time-gap between passing cars. Just along from my gaff they were still building the Hyatt Hotel on the site where *The Rum Runner* used to be. I could usually hear the clanking and drilling construction work starting about eight most mornings. The club used to be all neon lights and mirrored columns. Duran Duran was the house band before they hit the big time. Loads of pop stars of the day hung out there. Myself, I hadn't been in there since about 1986, when I got chucked out for rubbing Gorgonzola sauce in Limahl's hair. To much gnashing of teeth and lamentation amongst its regular drinkers, they started knocking the place down towards the end of 1987. Good riddance to bad rubbish, I say. Although memories of *The Rum Runner* are frequently discussed all over the city and beyond, I hated the place. Fucking Poseurs Palace. For some of us, the place isn't the legend it's made out to be. It was chock-full of posing, pretentious New Romantic fairies. But I suppose that was the thing at the time. And I, of course, was never part of the thing.

I got outta bed and spat a glob of thick, dark blood in the basin. The morning felt like nothing at all. Desolate. Like wind whistling through a rusty old tin can. I'm suddenly edging towards the end now. My flesh and bone matter decaying by the second, veins stabbed, rotten, lifeblood dripping from the wounds inflicted on me by the life I alone have chosen.

It comes back to me. I'm no one. I'm just another social security number. A piece of data printed out on a government computer that identifies me as a tax-paying subject of the state: rubber stamped – Mark Karzoso: DECEASED.

Spiral Out

I have no place in time. Youth is so fleeting. I'm watching beauty get old. Every day I am watching everything I had ever known wither away right before my eyes. Nothing is the same any more; we so desperately linger on past glories like faded old actors, like a tree blackened by lightning. It's all for nothing in the end, pointless. You end up in the ground and it's as simple and final and arbitrary as that.

Sometimes it occurs to me that it's the little things that are beyond our control. Like your vocal chords. It's something to do with the diameter of your vocal chords and how air is permitted to filter through them that sets your tone of voice. Some people are born in such a way they have a velvet tone of voice, something people find attractive. I don't, I have an obnoxious voice that grates on people's nerves. We're all puppets in this warped dance of marionettes. And some cunt somewhere is pulling the strings.

The joke is I was born on the right side of the tracks. Into easiness. It was 1989 now. The whole of the past decade had for me been riotous. I could remember twisted, discoloured faces viewed through a haze of acid or ecstasy or speed, occasional inconsequential moments in bars or nightclubs that for some reason had lodged in my mind. Little things here and there, seen in flash-back mode like a fuzzy VHS tape on fast rewind. I could see frozen images. But I couldn't recall the real, emotional essence of my experiences, that one aspect that is so

Spiral Out

essential in making us human.

I used to think I was born of a generation hell-bent on self-destruction. But after a time I realised I wasn't. It was just me and others of my ilk.

My apartment was on the corner where Granville street joins Broad Street. A swish city pad on the second floor, I had a view of Broad Street, past the Hyatt site and all the way up to Paradise Circus. My family owned a diamond merchants in the city's Jewellery Quarter over in Hockley. I wasn't ashamed to say I didn't work. I lived off an allowance, a handout from my parents. Spent most days skulking about behind my Venetian blinds. In the nineteenth century young men like me were referred to as a "private gentleman" – in other words: the idle rich. I never really understood the term *dream job*. How could anyone have a dream job? It completely dumbfounded me that anyone not only wanted to work their guts out but actually felt passionate about it. If everyone, the whole nation, just woke up tomorrow morning and refused to roll out of bed the government would surely be powerless to do anything about it.

As I see it, money is the wage of slavery. It is how they keep you trampled under the hooves of the king's mount. If you don't believe me try telling the tax man to go fuck himself, from now on you're gonna print your own money. See what happens there.

Most people are born into shit. They're born into a life

of prescribed anti-depressants and benefit payments. A quagmire of absolute hopelessness that is almost impossible to fight their way out of. And what defined them was how well they mauled their way through all the shit.

I had nothing to define me. There was nothing I had any desire to strive for. My life was just untainted white noise with me staring blankly at the screen. Here's love and hope, and here's the gutter: take your pick. I had wilfully chosen the gutter.

We were on our weekly trip to the bank. I was holding my mother's hand. She'd just deposited a wad of money when three men in black balaclavas burst in and the one gripping a shotgun ordered everyone to lie down. It was 1966. The bank manager himself, a man in a blue suit, with thinning silver hair, leapt over his desk and tried to take one of the men on, grappling with him. He seemed strong, too, and appeared to be over-powering his masked adversary. But the bank-robber produced some kind of blade and slit the manager's throat. He slumped to the floor, the blood spilled everywhere and as it spread further out, turning the grey carpet dark red, all three raiders escaped with bags of cash. I was five years old and didn't even understand what was going on.

- is the manager man going to get up mom? I asked anxiously.

- no son   she said picking me up and turning my face away from the dying man   not this   time.

It all stayed with me and as I got older the experience further compounded my stance that nothing matters at all. And nothing, neither love nor money, is worth caring about. The authorities' most decisive victory over the masses is having convinced them a life of hard, ball-breaking work is a virtue.

Through circumstance I'd fallen on the right side of the tracks and easiness had helped blend the lethargic ingredients of who I'd become. But my experiences confirmed my suspicions.

There have always been those who have proclaimed themselves the fucked-up generation. Of course, I realised that was bullshit. No generation is fucked up. It's just the ones like me, who lack the temerity to envision anything beyond their own self-infused indolence. I had set out with the intention of nullifying my own life.

If there were happy times during my childhood I don't remember them. I never fitted in anywhere and nothing struck me as worth fighting for. The kids at school were cruel. My nickname was Flid. I was about eleven years old when that started and that hurt me enough for me to just try and forget about it, to say nothing and bury it within myself. You can only play the cards life deals you, so you wear a poker face. I disconnected my feelings from everyone else. But when it comes right down to it, it's all only a charade, and in pretending I buried a poisoned seed that was to germinate inside me. I turned everything inwards. When I left school drink and drugs became my only friend, my retreat. There was never an umbilical cord between me and the rest of humanity.

5

The phone rang. I hadn't heard Offenbach mentioned in a couple of years. And I hadn't heard off my dad for weeks, possibly months. I dunno; I frequently lose track of time. It wasn't anything unusual, even growing up I didn't see much of either of my parents – they were always off working, building this empire we have today. I was pretty much left to my own devices growing up, I lacked all guidance. Not because they were bad parents, they were just ambitious in their pursuits. But my dad wanted me to go over to his office to meet him and Offenbach. Said there was something he needed me to be in on.

He still had delusions that I'd be running the place one day and sometimes thought there was a side to operations I should be aware of. He wanted me to watch and learn. Just keep your mouth shut because you've got a stupid mouth and observe how I deal with this, he was always instructing. So later that morning there I am standing in my father's plush leather and wood office all punctual like, wearing a fur coat, torn Levi 501's and high Cuban heels.

Karzoso Snr saw a spider crawling across his desk. He bought down his glass of malt whisky and crushed the unfortunate creature.

> - today he said plopping down at his desk ill be dealing with a little problem weve been having i want you to take a seat in the corner over there and watch how this is done youre not going to be a loafer forever one day you may well be warming this chair yourself *fucking god forbid*! He rolled his eyes upwards.

With a flourish dad adjusted his gold cuff links on his crisp white shirt and buzzed his secretary.

> - send in Offenbach he ordered sternly.

He sank down in his leather wing-backed chair and smoothed his hands over his slicked back grey hair. Yeah, my dad was a flash bastard. He impressed me sometimes.

Offenbach was tall but otherwise unassuming, he'd affected the appearance of a low-level bank clerk with his polished brogues and parted hair. Invisibility. I'd imagine that was the key to the nature of his business. You wouldn't think there was anything different about him. Despite his high earnings he drove only a bland, grey Nissan Sunny. He breezed through the door and leaned his dripping black umbrella against the wall in the corner of the room. He unbuttoned his dark suit jacket and sat down self-assuredly, relaxing into the soft leather chair opposite my dad, crossing his legs.

On the oak desk between them were piles of papers and one of those chrome perpetual motion executive toys – a tightrope walker holding a barbell that swayed back and forth.

- coming straight to the point   Karzoso Snr said stirring the ice cubes around in his drink with his finger   i think youre aware that we have someone within our organisation who is   shall we say compromising our structural integrity   he offered the bottle to Offenbach.

- no thank you   Offenbach held up his hand   to be specific you mean the Bulgarian connection   i believe youre referring to a certain Michel Bertrand character?

- indeed Mr Offenbach   our problematic Bulgarian connection   as you already know we will shortly be making an important step forwards in the companys evolution and i want you to see to it that Michel Bertrand   this irritant if you will   is removed from the equation.

- you want me to ermm   manage him out of the business?

Karzoso Snr laughed and said with wave of his hand:

- i like your way of putting it even better yes i want you to manage him out of the business   as cleanly as possible with no ripples left on the surface of the pond.

- and what kind of remuneration are we talking about?

- you get ten grand upon completion   any additional personal expenses youre likely to incur can be paid up front if youd prefer but i only pay the ten when the job is done.

Offenbach's lips curled downwards, he made a quick weighing scales gesture with his hands,

- ill require a few days to begin travel preparations of

Spiral Out

course   then ill need some time over there to study the form and assess the situation before piecing together a plan of action.

- i don't give a shit how you do it Mr Offenbach   dad drained his Scotch and slammed the glass down   but ive got a three million quid consignment of hot rocks being distributed in   just six month's time so i do want a swift and clean conclusion you understand   the Karzoso Diamond Company cant accommodate such free radicals in its midst not at this time   not at any time this is a tight ship and it cant stay afloat any other way if we are not careful this bastards gonna get the lot of us all nicked!

- no problem you know ill get the job done   but one other thing   ill also need a long holiday afterwards   on you Mr Karzoso   i want to go somewhere nice   some place warm   with palm trees and a golf course   ill need to disappear for a while   i need to practice my swing   could we say florida perhaps?

- sure ill even throw in a bottle of sun tan oil and a set of clubs   dad gave one of his twisted smiles.

Spiral Out

The two associates stood up and shook hands. Offenbach reached over and offered me his hand as well, giving me the customary nod as he did so. Then he buttoned up his suit before collecting his umbrella and walking out the room. As he was half through the door he turned and gave a little salute, adding sharply:

- ill be in touch.

Dad poured us both another shot and scraped the remains of the dead spider off the bottom of his cut glass tumbler along the edge of the desk. He had a business empire that stretched from here in Birmingham, England to the USA, Canada and South Africa. This new Bulgarian contract would form the hub of his operations for the next two years and he wasn't about to let some little Flemish upstart jeopardise that, he said venomously. He buzzed through to reception again,

- Louise if anyone asks no one has been in here to see me today.

Loosening his tie dad walked over and stood looking out the window. Who did some of these little bastards think they were dealing with? To know that such a life as Michel Bertrand's has ceased breathing whilst one continues to live:

Spiral Out

this is to have succeeded. We must crush our enemies completely, leave no smouldering embers left alive, he spat.

- you still writing that novel of yours son?

- here and there but theres nothing much to write about.

- you read much poetry Tennyson for instance?

- not really.

- what all that private education i shelled out for you and you dont read any Tennyson? a master at his game but he knew jack shit about fuck all   let me tell you something this isnt a world for poets Mark   Tennyson said love is the only gold   well you let the poets take all the love they can get while you take all the gold   always go with the gold son trust me love will only break you in half   he waggled his finger   let there be no room for it in your heart   its nothing but a disease that softens a man up   turns him to mush and kills him from within.

The Hockley streets were swarming, as always; full of

Spiral Out

people buzzing about doing their dodgy dealing, hiding their true selves behind small-talk and smiles. Dad shook his head in a kind of introspective dismay. If there was any other way to deal with this, he would have done so.

> \- its just fucking disgusting the way you cant trust anyone these days   he said flicking out his tongue as if he'd tasted something unpleasant.

> \- well i spose money can break your heart too   I suggested   or at least the pursuit of it?

Dad spun around suddenly from the window to face me.

> \- i wish youd smarten yourself up look at you fucking disgrace go on fuck off to wherever youre going get out of my sight you could go and get your hair cut but i suppose youre spending your day drifting about as usual?

> \- this is how i dress dad   I shrugged   hey you couldnt see your way clear to lending us a tenner could you? I joked.

> \- well dont come here again looking like that   you look

Spiral Out

like a girl   this is a business im running here and youre a damned embarrassment   no i cant lend you a tenner you cheeky little bastard fuck off.

As I was about to leave my dad called me back and stuffed his hand in his pocket.

- Mark   son   do you need a tenner really?

- nah just winding you up.

He blew heavily through his lips like a horse and waved me away impatiently,

- get out   he snapped.

I drove over to Mosley and went for a couple of lunchtime drinks at The Fighting Cocks. I didn't like Colin, the barman. He was a right-on fucker in an orange sweater down to his knees and filthy ginger dreadlocks who always bleated on about human rights issues. Colin was the type of man I refer to as a *Vagina-mouth*. Like all those of his ilk Colin wants the world to be a certain way so much that he is blind to unequivocal truths demonstrated time and time again throughout the history of mankind.

Vagina-mouth [vuh-jahy-nuh – mou*th*] noun, adj. A panty-waisted, lily-livered male afflicted with the disease of timidity, afraid to speak his mind for fear of people not liking him.

I laughed into my beer.

But still, despite Colin wanting to talk about political oppression in Palestine, I sat at the bar tolerating his chatter and one drink led to another and then I ended up not wanting to stop so I headed back into town and did a little afternoon tour of the bars by myself: The Pot of Beer >> The Black Horse >> Sinatra's >> West End Bar. I finally drove home shit-faced again, dumped the Merc in the lot at the back of the apartment block and fucked off to bed at 6pm to sleep the bastard off.

6

Marvin Starkie works at drive-thru joint just down the street from here, he doesn't give a shit about building you the best burger you've ever tasted; he's just trying the only way he can to get through the day. And the customers don't even know the fucking difference anyway. You could wipe humanity, every one of us, off the face of the earth and it wouldn't really matter

Spiral Out

a jot. The only thing a man has is time and that is taken from him. Only through a meaningful death does your life have any real significance. Most choose to cling to their meaningless existence instead, with little option but to flip burgers or clean bird shit of statues or whatever the fuck they have to do to scratch out a living. No matter how dull their lives are, suicide is not an option. Me, I do not work. I am heir to the Karzoso Diamond fortune and I believe that suicide is an act of brave insurrection.

Anyway, Marv came round. As soon as I opened the door he ducked down under the door-frame, darted in and bolted straight for the bathroom and locked the door. He was holed up in there for so long that I tapped on the door a couple of times without response. But after about an hour he came stumbling out, half bent over, holding his cramped stomach saying *fuckin hell that was like shittin a baby elephant*. I think it was a Saturday afternoon. I met Marv some time previous through someone else around town. I was looking to score some speed and some kid, whose name I've forgotten and who is now most likely dead, said he knew one of the old punks who'd be able to sort me out so we got in my car and he directed me over to the Castle Vale estate where Marvin lived in one of the few houses built on the estate tucked in amongst the many crumbling tower blocks.

Spiral Out

- you wanna rocket ride you gotta put some fuel in the tank   Marvin said dropping my supply of speed on the coffee table   know whaam sayin?

Yeah, I knew.
He'd also got this little bottle of stuff. I asked him what the fuck it was.

- ketamine man   he replied with a twisted smile jiggling the bottle of liquid before my eyes   this is the fuckin shit man   the real McCoy   laboratory grade horse-fuckin-tranquiliser   this stuff will blow your fuckin socks off man.

- that stuffs probably the reason for your constifuckingpation I said.

- dont talk wet Marv shook his head this stuff dont give you no constipation its medicinal compound medical grade stuff   get me?

- so?

- so it dont give you constipation its pure as the driven snow nah it musta been eatin that shit at work.

Spiral Out

Marvin tells me when he first started flipping burgers for this global fast food company he had to work his way through an induction They told him he'd be learning the company's ten fundamental, defining principles. He was to absorb them so that he could live and breathe them. That was the company's actual terminology: he was to *live and breathe* the company ethos. Live and breathe each and every fat-soaked, stinking crock-of-shit marketing lie. He was to become a better man; defined by their set of principles. Fucking jokers. He'll never let the bastards suck his spirit of all vitality. Because that's what they try to do in order to render you more malleable. To turn you into a robot.

> - nothin screams bullshit   Marv nods ardently   like being *told* to scream it while some fuckers threatenin to cut your balls off with a cheese wire.

He reckons it's fucking disgusting how these days your place of work is allowed to carry out drug and alcohol tests, like your job is your identity and you don't have no right to a personal life. What the fuck is it to them if you're fucked-up every night of the week so long as you do your job? The fuckers are in league with these fascist bastard governments. A demoralised populace, devoid of all hope, is an easy to control

Spiral Out

populace. All this fucking work really does not need to be done. When the day comes they pull Marvin Starkie in for one of their random drug tests he knows he can kiss the job goodbye. But who gives a flying fuck? He's not about to compromise his personal virtues; when man becomes a slave to global corporations the rout of civilisation has begun, Marvin spits his words out like he's tasted ammonia.

> - you know i got this friend   Marv is telling me school teacher   she tells me that as soon as them schoolgirls hit the legal age of sixteen them male teachers are sniffing round em like ravenous bees around a fuckin honey pot   more often than youd think it happens before   theyre sixteen   these teachers they do a lot of fuckin their pupils an all the others they all know its going on but rarely do they say anythin and the powers that be are more   concerned about a workin man like me smokin a bitta blow   you like cars so you become a racin driver or a mechanic   you like fiddlin with kids bits   you become a teacher   its fuckin obvious   its just rudimentary knowledge man   the whole system is fucked.

Marvin Starkie is the only friend I've got. He talks like this all the time. I mean, I call him a friend but really he just

Spiral Out

comes around here in his old, flea-bitten Ozric Tentacles teeshirt to sell me a bit of gear and dispense various nuggets of random information before fucking off again. He's unbelievably tall, about six-foot-eight with thick, black, cropped hair and elongated limbs and torso like those looming figures in Byzantine art. With his dense bones he carries with him a heavy presentiment of physical threat. His cheek-bone had been busted at some time and he had a scar on his cheek where they'd inserted a metal plate to reconstruct his face. But his eyes are very blue and convey a sense of compassion. They twinkle in the light and look like they have been transplanted from an altogether gentler human being. And I suppose he was gentle really. It was only his appearance. I don't recall ever seeing him actually perpetuating violence.

He gesticulates very little when he speaks and has developed the paranoid habit of talking conspiratorially out the corner of his mouth as he shares his knowledge on all matters, determined that no one else outside his circle of acquaintances somewhere might lip-read him. This one time I'm sitting in the armchair and he's lying on his back on the sofa, his long, drainpipe legs in black jeans dangling over the end. He's telling me that he's spotted a gap in the market. He's gonna pull up a van outside pubs on a Saturday night selling hot, buttered sprouts. He sparks up a joint, stabs the air with it and laughs his throaty laugh,

Spiral Out

- we dont sell fuckin cheeseburgers pal   its hot buttered sprouts and thats it   no sauce no chips no fuckin apple pies   just cones of beautiful HOT BUTTERED SPROUTS!

Marvin's joking, I think, smoking the joint through the gap where his front tooth used to be. What can I say? When all is said and done, Marvin is one of the happiest people I know. I wish I could be more like him; he really doesn't give two shits about anything. All he really wants is to win the Littlewoods Pools and go and live in Italy with the woman of his dreams. He fancies one of those brightly painted, crumbling little side-street villa things with shutters up the windows and a balcony where you can sit watching dusky sunsets over a little Italian market square. That's Marvin's little dream scenario.

Being ensconced in a Mediterranean villa with a woman is not a notion I can relate to. I have found women to be lying, manipulative, conniving bitches. I tell Marvin about how Lydia was so toxic if you liquidised her in a blender you could use her as tree-stump killer. Man, he replies, you have some fucked-up thoughts you do, Karzoso. And then he thinks for a moment, shakes his head and adds with a knowing raise of his eyebrows,

Spiral Out

- but any man who sez that sorta thing loves them too much for his own good.

7

After Marvin left, before going out to a café, I emptied a wrap of speed into a cigarette paper, twisted it up and bombed it. I did for a while consider carbon monoxide poisoning. But I didn't quite have the constitution for that so as a cowardly alternative I set out to destroy myself in other ways, to crucify what I have become with drink and drugs in the hope that something else from deep inside can emerge, Christ-like from the dead ashes, resurrected. That's the thing about the syringe. Like a bayonet, it is so pure. So unambiguous in its explicit intentions. I always thought there was something intensely erotic about sharing the drug taking ritual with a woman, the penetration of the blood vessels, the orgasmic waves of ecstasy.

In the mirror I ran a hand over my carved out, sunken cheeks. I'd always been alone in a private hell and shooting up my veins to kingdom-come was the only solution as I could see it. The old stone gods are dead. And now it was time to execute the angels that survived somewhere deep inside me so that I could finally be devoid of all emotion. The human machine is not unlike other technologies. As each new generation gets taller, better educated, more resistant to viruses that bother human beings the previous generation becomes defunct, a relic. With each new generation we are becoming less and less human as we currently know it. One day we will be part man and part unfeeling machine, we will turn our emotions on and off as we please. Roll on, I say, the day of the machines.

I left my apartment. The roads stretched in all directions, originating from nowhere and leading only to other dilapidated, colourless cities. It's the same all over. Perched on a lamp-post a crow, like a kindred spirit, screamed out his own personal agony. I looked to see from which direction the sun was rising but the landscape and sky were like two dark grey sheets of iron seamlessly welded together. Rain started to sweep over the streets.

I walked around in a trance, getting soaked for over an hour before going to a greasy spoon in Digbeth across the road from the National Express station.

Frowning from beneath her dainty little striped paper hat, the server shovelled a load of chips onto a plate and dumped a frayed glob of battered fish on top.

- you want ketchup?

- yeah I nodded and watched as she squirted too much of the stuff all over the already soggy offerings.

Spiral Out

Sometimes, as a form of camouflage, I just did things to appear normal. I did things I thought normal people might do. Sometimes I feigned acceptance of their inadequacies and even nodded and laughed along with them.

There was a gaggle of young mothers in there with their pre-school offspring who were banging spoons on tables, rolling on the floor squealing and throwing food about without a word of correction from their scabby parents, all of the mothers with cigarettes stuck in their mouths. I can't stand to be around them. The stench of their presence pervades my nostrils and coats my tongue with some vile, foetid mixture. One of the women was pregnant to the hilt, about to drop another stinking sprog into the world at any given moment. As I fork some of the fish in my mouth she gets to her feet and stands with hands on hips staring down at her kid rolling about the floor with jam smudged all over his face, her bulbous, red pregnant belly track marked with thick, purple and blue veins punches out from beneath a rising jumper. I almost throw up. Fuck off and stand somewhere else while people are trying to eat you piece of filthy fucking human garbage.

Are there really people like me? People that simply don't need anyone else? To me, the whole concept of sharing your life with another person seems a strange thing. I mean starting a family, lying in a stinking bed, waking up and eating fried breakfast with the same person day in, day out. I couldn't think of anything more depressing than working a nine-five job every single day and returning home to the clanking of pots and the scraping of plates, or the monotonous hum of the vacuum cleaner, spending every night sitting lethargically in a comfortable little corner of the living room imbibing all the crap on TV whilst eating toxic frozen foods that give people cancer. Every single day. Who wrote the rules that established all this part of convention? And why the fuck do so many find solace in living that kind of life? The whole physical process of giving birth, all the blood and bile and screaming, struck me as one of the most utterly horrific things you could witness. If Trevor Bayliss wanted to make a difference to the human race he shouldn't have invented the clockwork radio – he should have invented a clockwork abortion machine. The very sight of a baby and their mothers' kissing and slurping all over them fills me with a sense of repulsion.

    In the corner there was a couple holding hands over the table. The date was not recorded. The weather was cool and overcast with a light south-westerly wind and somewhere on the A38 to Lichfield a driver was killed today when his Ford Sierra ploughed into the back of an articulated truck. And meanwhile, someone's laundry tumbles inside one of the washing machines in a back-street launderette. And it doesn't matter a jot how much in love the couple in the café were because their love is ultimately inconsequential and any children they might have will amount to nothing and one day both of them will be ashes in the ground and the universe will not record any of these tiny moments in history at all.

I had to get out of there. Still perched on his post outside the crow watched me with his sharp, spurious eye through the window surreptitiously stir another wrap of Gonzales into my now cold coffee and swill it back. I saved him a couple of chips and tossed them to him when I walked out.

8

Marvin turned up at my flat later that night and brought this little weaselly fellow with him called Six Dogs. Six Dogs was a strange little fucker in a zipped-up blue Kagool and a huge torn and battered top hat that he told me was his party hat. He stood about five-foot-two and with that hat and his black jeans tucked into eighteen-hole Dr. Marten boots he looked to me like a creature out of Alice in Wonderland. He had an Exploited teeshirt on under the Kagool. I subsequently realised he didn't own any other clothes than these; they were all he ever wore. Six Dogs' face was a mass of scars and deep, jagged tramlines and, since he had an aversion to water, the scars were always ingrained with dirt. He said he'd been outta the scene for a while. Clucking. Doing cold turkey. It didn't work. He convinced himself he could over-see his own rehabilitation and stopped going to the doctor. He sourced his own methadone and then before he knows it he's got both the methadone and the H. Back to square fucking one. Six Dogs had been sectioned in a mental hospital a couple of times. He'd given up all hope of even trying to get off the Skag and came back to Birmingham but now almost everyone he'd known was dead and he barely recognised the place. But he and Marv went back a long way. They were two of the old-school punks off the 'Vale.

Six Dogs was thirty-six years old and lived in a one bed flat in a tower block on the degenerating Castle Vale estate. He didn't have any family. I suppose those old-school punks off the 'Vale he so often reminisced about became his only family. There used to be a whole gang of them, he said, most of whom were now dead. Neither was Six Dogs gainfully employed in any real capacity. He walked over and stood with his hands in his pockets and looked at my old *Velvet Underground* poster framed on the wall and promptly told me he was a band manager. I asked him what bands he managed, thinking he might mention one of the ones that were making a name for themselves on the Birmingham scene at the time like *Birdland* or *The Filipinos*. But the three bands he revealed that were on

Spiral Out

his books were nothing of the kind: *Superboy Fuckmuff*, *The Fat Ginger Kids*, and his personal favourite – a band he predicted big things for – *Undescended Testicle*. I'd never heard of any of them.

Six Dogs kept jerking his head and at first I thought he was flicking his straggly, shoulder-length hair out of his face but he wasn't. It was a nervous tick. He really was just a bag of fucked. Marvin told me Six Dogs was abandoned at birth, found whimpering, naked in a cardboard box, discarded on a rubbish tip. Marv thought this was probably the reason Six Dogs latched onto people the way he did.

> - once hes in your life   Marv said   youll never get rid of him   he sticks to you like glue   thats how he gets his name   story goes he wuz sniffed out and raised during his formative years by a packa stray dogs before being taken into some kind of care institution   jokey stories aside when you get a start like that in life you got no chance brother.

By all accounts Six Dogs was not given to violence but he did like to rob off-licencies and pharmacies as a way of sustaining himself when an opportunity arose.

The fact was we needed to score and Marvin said we should get down Los Mangos Café over in Lozells and see the

Spiral Out

Priest. Six Dogs says *The Fat Ginger Kids* are playing Edwards No' 8 club next week and he wants to make sure he's got enough supplies in to make a night of it. They've apparently got an appointment to meet this Priest character. So Marvin's wearing his business gear: black wraparound sunglasses, a red track-suit top with stripes down the arms, black drainpipe jeans and big, steel-toe-capped boots. He's combed his thick black hair and it looks like *Mr. Spock's*.

Los Mangos was almost exclusively a blacks' joint. You wouldn't normally go there but ultimately everyone got their drugs off the blacks. That's just the reality of such matters whether people want to admit it or not.

Priest was said to be the hardest man in Birmingham. He used to drink in another criminal riddled pub called the Witch Elm but no longer went there since blowing the landlord's fingers off with a shotgun during a mass brawl.

More cash for narcotics swapped hands in Los Mangos than it ever did for drink. For a while a broken gas pipe spewed flames into the bar and the regulars had entertained themselves by setting fire to most of the furniture. There used to be a juke box in the corner until somebody fucking nicked it.

Six Dogs came waltzing back out of the bathroom looking quite pleased with himself, his stringy brown hair sticking to his dirty face and says:

Spiral Out

- we boys gonna goo up an get this gear or wha?

- the lady will havta put her make up on first   Marvin smirked nodding in my direction.

I ignored him and quickly traced on my black eye-liner in the mirror propped up on the mantle piece. I put on my black jeans and rock n roll tiger print crepe shoes.

- thats it   done shitface   I said giving Marvin the finger.

When Six Dogs laughed his head twitched even more and the sound that came out of his mouth was like the anguished squawk of a crow.

9

The Priest's Yamaha TZR250 is sticking out like a sore thumb, parked on the pavement outside the window. Priest is not like the other blacks in there. Next to it was a jazzed-up purple Ford Capri 2.8i with big silver wheels and elevated rear suspension; *Raggamuffin General* plastered across the back window in big gold letters. We'd jumped on a bus over to

Spiral Out

Lozells, what Marvin referred to as the African Quarter. It was raining when we got off and we walked the deprived streets up to Los Mangos. I had no intention of parking the 350SL anywhere in any street in Lozells. They'd swoop down like the fucking vultures they are. There'd be fuck-all left of it.

The stench of a hundred different cheap colognes blending together drifts out the door and hangs in the air on the corner outside the bar, mixing with exhaust fumes and the strong aroma of marijuana as traffic crawls along the Lozells Road with pumping music almost blowing out their car windows.

It's still only 8 pm and the drunks have already spilled raging out onto the street, fists swinging. Droplets of blood spatter the pavement. A Rastafarian lays face down beaten unconscious or dead, rainwater gushes along the gutter and swills a gallon of blood from a gash in his head down a drain. They leave him there. No one calls police or ambulances around these parts. And when they do call the police it's only to lure them into a trap where they'd wait with baseball bats.

It's a typical Saturday night at Los Mangos Café. The furniture in there is all bolted to the floor so no fucker can pick it up and break it over your head. There was one occasion when some white guy walked in of a lunchtime and asked Al if it would be alright if he brought his teenage daughter in just to use the toilet.

Spiral Out

- its your daughter its your daughters virginity   Al warns the guy with a shrug.

Far be it from me to cast aspersions but I'd have to agree with Al. You only have to look at them. These fucking Neanderthals got arms down to their knees and probably a constant boner. It's a known fact they cannot control their animalistic impulses in the same way as we whites do.

It's called a café but they don't exactly serve coffee and cakes. It stinks of ganja. A gaseous mix of yellow smoke pervades the air, tinged purple in the spot lights, like the cloud nebula. Paint peels from the walls. Dread-locked blacks hover around with watchful glares. They prowl the bar like panthers, show their gold teeth and eyeball you with suspicion, like they're gonna tear you apart, like you're never gonna to make it outta the place alive. They babble on aggressively in some strange language so you can never understand a word they say to each other. Fuck knows what it is. It isn't Jamaican Patois, even though that's what people usually call it. It isn't that. You only know the bastards are talking about your presence in there. But I garnered enough to know the top-dog in Los Mangos was a hulking six-foot-four Rasta called Keldo.

A foreboding sense of threat saturates the place with all the cantankerous despondence of a pig awaiting slaughter. The

Spiral Out

only thing I will say for the place is nobody smiles. And one thing I'd learned from growing up around my father's business acquaintances was that you don't trust people who smile too much. But these fuckers were too base and stupid to know how to use any kind of psychology. I notice that apart from being white, with his long, thick bones and sulky brow, Marvin Starkie doesn't look an inch out of place in there, especially with that curved scar down his cheek. He knows everyone, greets them by doing that black-brother thing of punching fists together.

    We found Priest sitting over in the corner. He's big and bald. As black as coal with a big, gnarled broken nose; F.U.C.K and T.I.T.S tattooed across the knuckles of each hand, only faintly visible because he's so dark skinned. He's got a sidekick known as Hot Toes sitting next to him, a small and skinny vicious looking bastard who eyed me suspiciously with the darting, silvery eyes of a pigeon, cigarette tucked behind his right ear. Hot Toes had just done a ten-year stretch for blagging a Securicor van. His face seemed to be frozen in an everlasting paranoid grimace. We walked over to the table and Priest called me a Muppet, made some predictable wisecrack about no women being allowed in the place, and instructed me to fuck off and wait at the bar; he said the men over here needed to talk business. Hot Toes yanked the cigarette from behind his ear, put it in his mouth and stared me down with a misshapen grin, itching for me to commit some transgression so he could kick off. I am an anachronism to him, the kind of person outside his experience or understanding and he thus found me being there extremely offensive to his own being. I reached into my pocket and handed Marv my share of the deal.

    I relaxed onto a stool at the bar and ordered a shot of whisky. Not surprisingly, Al doesn't have any proper whisky glasses so the drink sat paltry-like at the bottom of a greasy finger-marked pint glass. Al is short for Alfonso or summat like that. He's Mexican or Panamanian or Puerto Rican or something. He is wearing a red bandanna and an eye-patch over his cock-eye. A while ago one of his customers smashed a bottle in his face, costing him the eye.

    While I'm waiting for the men over there to conduct their business one of the Rastas with a thick scar across his face, built like a brick shit-house, wearing a pair of mirror aviators motioned with his hand and shouted over:

- yo batty bwoy.

Then he gets up from where he was sitting on the edge of the red-baized pool table, making a little performance of it, and saunters over and grabs me by the hair, yanking my head back. A strong smell of weed wafted in his wake.

Spiral Out

- you is a whitebwoy dressed as a bitch or you is a bitch dressed as a whitebwoy? he glared mockingly at me.

I stared back and thought how cool I looked, fish-eyed in his lenses, like the cinematography you see in those seventies American cop films on teevee. The rest of his posse all fell about laughing, waddling about, grabbing their crotches and all that stupid shit these people do. I wanted to reply: *why? you looking for a piece of ass, black boy?* But it was really better to say fuck all. These niggers were much more sensitive about these things than we are. Because of their lower social status they have an inferiority complex, less confidence in themselves, and because of that they'll over-compensate. They strut down the street with that fuck you look in their eyes, propping up a fragile identity with false posturing. And, trust me, they'll stick a blade in you for as much as looking at them.

Part of the problem was that these people lacked identity; so they were in a kind of arrested development, like life-long teenagers searching for who they are, and in doing so they have to form these little tribes. I hated school but thank fuck I went to private schools, places these second class citizens couldn't afford to go, and I didn't have to associate with them growing up. There were no blacks at the schools I went to. There were no poor white kids either. But I did

Spiral Out

understand one thing and that is that we are all random creations. Fragile by design, we are subject to dysfunction. Even nationality is an illusion that traps us. National identity is bullshit. That wars have been fought over these illusions of identity is the pinnacle of our weakness as a species. We are all unavoidably born into a tribe of some sort, separated only by financial status.

We are each lost and ultimately alone in the universe. Everything we do stems from a need to fulfil this loneliness, to look into the void and ask: is there no one else like me, no one else who understands the mechanisms of my world? And yet, we defend what we think we are, sometimes to the point of death, to the point of war. We fight to preserve the illusion of our existence. Our opinions and thoughts provide us with a self-sufficient delusion of who we think we are and we try to impose that identity upon the material universe. But I always thought too much, a prisoner in my own hell. I needed a drink to free me.

I picked up my pint glass of whisky, downed it in one and turned to expel whisky fumes in the nigger's face like a motherfucker.

At that moment Keldo snapped his fingers and motioned for his minion, who he referred to as Colbow, to leave me alone. Colbow obeyed and loosened his grip -- but spat in my face before walking away. No doubt the substitute

Spiral Out

ejaculate of a closet homosexual. What he really subconsciously wanted to do was smash my back doors in and he didn't even know it.

No one moved in on their turf in Los Mangos. But Priest was moving in on their turf with blatant impunity. Even the Yardies were wary of Priest and his cohorts. They knew he was tooled up. But sooner or later he had it coming. When the right time came one of them would do him good and proper. You don't go to war with these people. It looked like Priest thought he'd got Keldo running scared but I doubted there was any chance of that. Priest may well have been a big fish in his own pond but Keldo was just biding his time. I reckoned Keldo looked like he already knew the time and the place.

Priest laughed about the TV show *Roots,* at how one of its main characters was Kunta Kinte. For the last few weeks since he'd shifted camp he'd been trying to stamp his authority on Los Mangos by identifying the top boy and making a big show of ridiculing him, calling him Cunta Keldo and taking the piss out of his pimped-up ride.

- whys he got Raggamuffin General on the back winnda of that shit-box? Priest cackled from under his rock to the whole bar   when every man and his dog know his names Cunta Keldo?   At this Hot Toes laughs a grating, chesty laugh like he smokes ten packs of

Spiral Out

Woodbine's a day.

You still didn't see too many people prancing around with mobile phones in 1989. Keldo leaned cool as ice with his back against the bar, calmly tapping a number into his Motorola DynaTac. Those were like two grand or something when they first came out; more than the cunt's pimp-car was worth. Particles of dust floated in shafts of diffused light from the dirty windows. Like the alpha gorilla he stared into the middle distance, phone to his ear, nonchalantly ignoring the challenge to his authority. The only sign Priest's goading had registered was that Keldo sucked his teeth and whispered *boboleeee* under his breath, to someone on the other end of the phone. Keldo just carried an air of severe danger about him that signalled to everyone not to fuck with him. Whites of eyes flashed in Priest's direction, fierce looking flared nostrils, snorting like a bull.

By the looks of it the men in the corner were concluding their business. I watched Marvin, Hot Toes and Priest all shake hands in turn and Marvin stuffed the plump looking baggie in his jeans. Sorted.

Before they wrapped up their meeting for good I watched Priest grab hold of Six Dogs and smack him hard around the head a few times, he stabbed a finger in his face like he was giving him a warning of some kind. I heard him

Spiral Out

demand whatever it was - by the end of next week.

As we walked out of there Keldo grabbed my arm and leaned close to my ear.

- i seeved yaar skin today Battybwoy   but if ay see you in here ageen ay breek every one of your feengers meself   nowya fuck off mon. He let go of me with a shove.

10

- it seems a bit of a stupid name   I said as we cut fine figures of men walking back along the street to the bus stop   so why the fucks he called Priest anyway?

Marvin kind of flashed me his blue-eyed look sideways and said as if the answer should be obvious:

- cuz if you get on the wrong side of him youll be administered the last rites!

- that coon who spat in my face   I said changing the subject through gritted teeth   i shoulda knocked his black cock off.

Spiral Out

- get fucked Karzoso   Marv laughed showing the gap in his front teeth   if you was a red-indian your named be Fainting Possum you cunt.

He slapped me on the back and told me to relax, said no worries, we got what we went for, didn't we?

Six Dogs crowed until his face went purple, calling me Fainting Possum. He laughed until he hacked up a load of phlegm and spat it out onto the pavement and added absent mindedly, shaking his head:

- silver spoon boys.

We stood in the middle of the African Quarter, outside a filthy hovel of a Halal butcher shop with carcasses of rotten, black cows hanging in the windows. With his stooped over stance and little bandy legs Six Dogs' gait was rather like that of a little chimp. He punched the air with sudden gusto and said with uncharacteristic dynamism:

- *come on! lets do a fuckin off-licence over man!*

Spiral Out

11

The first time I goofed out on Heroin was four years before. 1985, it would have been. It was like sinking into a sea of warm marmalade. And once submerged in its sickly sweet balm I was cast adrift in a universe of dreams. And in the middle of vacant, non-existence I had found freedom. The outside world was no longer my enemy because my final tenuous connection with it had been severed forever. From that moment on I had found diamond seas on which to set sail, islands of bliss on which to dwell. It was like no other drug. From then on I thought: fuck reality. Fuck reality up the jacksie with a red-hot poker. A mathematician might tell you 2+2 don't add up to 4. And if you don't believe him he might tell you he'll write out an equation to prove it. I have no desire to argue the rudiments of existential existence. 2+2=4 and I have no desire to either understand why or change anyone else's perception of it.

None of my pontification mattered. In the future those groups of people who contrive to convince society that any criticisms levelled against them is prejudice are the ones who will control society itself. Once again it's all about manipulating illusions. In the real world you get hit around the back of the fucking swede with a house brick, it ain't never gonna feel like a marshmallow. It's a catch-22 situation:

Spiral Out

liberalism is the open door through which fascism walks. Stupid lefty cunts. We're living in a time when society is becoming afraid of words, afraid of thought; afraid of the simplest of words that make them think because they challenge mass delusions. And as far as I was concerned that's all there was to it. But To proclaim that you love life takes a modicum of bravery. And I was a born coward. I had tried all my life to be part of it all, sought the approval of the rest of the human race. But the world had rejected me and excluded me. I learned to hate the sun. I didn't give a shit. I wanted darkness to fall and never lift. I wanted to live forever in the corners of dark nightclubs, fucked out of my skull, my deformed image shifting unnoticed through the artificial mix of laser lights and dry ice.

Back at my Granville Street apartment I put *Holst: The Planets* on the stereo and Six Dogs heated the makeshift foil dish with a lighter while I sucked the emissions through a cardboard tube from the middle of a toilet roll. The initial rush knocked me back on the sofa, where I remained incapacitated, ecstatic, for I don't know how long. Every cell in my body pulsed like a fermenting atom gearing up to detonate and blow the last strands of my existence across the heavens. And I was too fucked to care. Too fucked to care that splattered across the firmament, blown to kingdom come, there would be no trace of me having ever existed at all. I felt like a God. I was

Spiral Out

omnipotent. I felt as though I could with a single scything thought have blown all the tower blocks around me away as if they were flimsy houses of cards. I could have opened wide my majestic arms and embraced the cosmos, and then crushed it to a muddy pulp between my hands. I was the final arbiter. I could have moulded new worlds out of clay. I was Mars the bringer of war! But I just couldn't be bothered to muster the energy.

And when you use Heroin that just about sums it up. The world is yours for the taking. But you're not even able to lift as much as a coffee cup. In my stupor I lay back and watched Six Dogs' blood ooze into the syringe, curling like red smoke. He carried his works with him in a leather zip-up case small enough to fit in his pocket. He waited a few seconds, as if savouring the sight of it, then blasted the mixture into the veins in his ankle. For a moment his face looked as though he was in the throes of orgasm. He let out a gasp of relief, the life-force magically returned to his face and he at once was human again. His flesh became reanimated and his yellow eyes transformed back to their usual sad-dog brown. It was like watching a corpse return to life.

Later on, as we were gluing ourselves together to make our way over to the Black Horse, Marvin holds up the bottle of the lab-grade Ketamine he's been holding onto and says *c'mon, it's time to let the genie out the bottle.* We shot it up and I was blasted out of my fuckin skull, man. The minute we did it all

Spiral Out

three of us dropped like dead donkeys. There was nothing left of me, I felt as though I'd been vaporised. I guess that's why they call it Donkey Dust. Took all three of us a while to regain control of our muscles and then Six Dogs realised he'd pissed himself. He took off his jeans and stood there in front of us, seemingly oblivious to how humiliating it was to be standing there drying the crotch of his jeans with my hair dryer. He had no underpants on. Never wore them, he bragged matter-of-factly when we laughed at him. He had a small, shrivelled penis paired with huge, sagging balls dangling between his bandy little legs. For the rest of the night we taunted him by calling him Nappy Rash.

    I went and stood over by the window. The night was so clear and the sky full of stars. So full of such scintillating bright, white stars glowing like some strange field of exotic flowers. I don't think I'd ever seen the stars so bright and I thought about how there is such beauty all around us, yet we just do not possess the power to harness it. Beauty in life is limited to these brief moments of sensory pleasure. And then it dissolves into the blankness once again.

    We walked down the street, me hiding behind my big, gold-framed Elvis sunglasses. We'd make it in time for last orders in the *Black Horse*, bang one or two cold ones back there, drop a couple of Strawberries, and then head on up to the *Hummingbird* nightclub. We'd walk in and the DJ'd be playing

Spiral Out

The Paris Angels or The Spacemen 3 and everyone sprawled all over the floor blasted out of their brains. That's how it was back then, before the police put the kibosh on the place, closed the joint down. Those were the days. After the place re-opened under new gaffers it was never the same again, they cleaned the place up and we thought it was shit. Students who nowadays have to pay their education fees back act all grown-up, standing about drinking fucking carrot juice and talking about their dreams of getting a job in a bank or some other institutionalised detention centre. It's all bullshit. We have become a nation of slaves in a vast bureaucracy. We are under the hoof. No such thing as success; for almost everyone there is only birth and death and the incalculable subservience in-between.

The last thing I remembered of the night before we all split up and lost each other was us three fine gentlemen striding past the Rotunda feeling great and not giving a fuck about no one. We continued down by the burger place Marv worked at, where the overweight, flatulent masses stuff themselves and their offspring full of cheeseburgers and fries. I can't believe there are high-chairs provided for babies in there. I wouldn't feed a child such utter fucking shite. You know, around Birmingham I'd seen people maimed, stabbed, shot, even beaten to death outside a kebab shop in an argument over a taxi at two o'clock in the morning. And I don't care a fuck about any of that. But it really makes my piss boil when I see these

Spiral Out

vile parents wilfully stuffing a cheeseburger into a baby's mouth. Fucking scum.

You only have to look through the windows of those places to see evidence of why such a large percentage of the populace should be exterminated. This is why nothing will ever change in the world. There will never be a revolution. That fighting spirit in man is dead. They could put a man on Mars and the mindless masses would just go back to sucking on their Mcdonalds and Coca-Cola. This is the global apocalypse, it has happened. But it didn't happen in the physical realm as anyone expected; it is an apocalypse of the mind. We are beaten good and proper now. Governments and corporations have won the war against their populaces. And they did it by using their own fucking foolish apathy against them. The authorities' most decisive victory was convincing everyone that hard work is some kind of virtue.

It gave me greater and greater pleasure, each day knowing I was an accomplice to it, that my brain was shot full of holes; walking around in a daze, barely able to remember anything and yet realising with increasing clarity that the drug addict is his own freedom fighter through an ever increasing sense of blissful disconnection. I am born of the narcotic generation. The generation that found an escape. And now that we have found our freedom, how do they like their young pin-eyed boys? It was always there for the taking and now their

Spiral Out

world is a dying sun.

Some drunken trendy guy who thinks he's Rick fucking Astley in wide, white cotton slacks and blue blazer looking for his fix tries the burger joint door and after trying to push the door when it says pull the thick fucker thinks it's closed so he kicks it angrily and gives it the finger before swerving his way down the street. He thinks the clothes make him look suave but they don't, they make him look like a poxy little twat. Next door there was a bearded old tramp in an alcohol induced coma, slumped in a doorway with vomit in his beard and all down his front. Six Dogs went over and without waking him up, tenderly pressed a quid in the palm of his hand. I suppose others might call it a touching moment. He didn't know the old tramp. And he never said anything about why he did it and neither Marv nor I said anything about it either. I do not begrudge the drifter his moment of release. If it weren't for privilege I too would be like that; a nowhere nothing fuck-up.

It started to rain again. Street lights reflected in the wet pavements as we walked along, under the bridge and past the Irish pub on the corner of Dale End. It's called something else now and I don't even recall what it was called then -- but I went there once to drink all afternoon before seeing the Ramones play the Hummingbird and I ended up barely able to remember a fucking thing about the gig but the next morning I'd got an autographed drumskin on the coffee table. So

Spiral Out

anyway, we crossed the road there, used the underpass beneath the James Watt Queensway, and cut across Aston university campus to the *Black Horse*.

I managed to pull some little blonde student bird in a short Tartan skirt and sexy Dr. Marten's boots somewhere along the line that night. And after we left a pub, somewhere wandering the streets, I ended up fucking her in a shop doorway. I still had my big, gold sunglasses on. When along walks this one, doing that arrogant, casual stroll that they do; swinging his handcuffs around his index finger. He comes to a halt with a very militaristic stomp of his boot and snaps:

- what the hell do you think youre doing?

- its all right officer   I say   we re only neckin.

- yeah   well put your neck back in your trousers then Elvis and fuck off home pronto before i arrest the pair of you.

12

I awoke face down on the cold lino in Marv's kitchen, the whole room flashing red / black / red / black / red /black.

Spiral Out

No idea how long I'd been lying there. No memory of anything after walking to the Black Horse. I remember walking in there and that's it. Shivering I dragged myself to my feet and steadied myself against a battered, bare metal washing machine, feeling like my spine had disintegrated. The room seemed to be disconcertingly slanted sideways at a forty-five degree angle. I looked in the fridge. It was empty apart from a can of Dr. Pepper and an open tin of congealed corned beef. I was so cold that when I put my hand in the fridge it felt warm. I snapped open the Dr. Pepper and drank it. My bones felt like soft rubber. I was diminishing into the ether.

There were muffled, indistinct voices and a TV blaring in the next room. One of the voices was Marvin's dull monotone, not really saying anything but just droning on and on like the continuous background hum of an old prop shaft.

Inclined against the wall in the corner of the kitchen was a cracked dress mirror. No frame. Traces of white powder spattered all over it. I looked at my reflection but almost didn't recognise the decrepit image staring back at me. My skin had taken on a sweating pale green hue and my dull eyes were hollow as two smoke ring halos. I was totally spent. My chest was tight and breathing difficult; I thought my heart was finally giving out or something. I had to consciously force myself to suck in air and let it out again.

On the sideboard I found a soft pack of odorous

Spiral Out

Chinese cigarettes with a child-like rendering of a panda bear on the front. I took one and lit it with the Swan Vesta's from my jeans' pocket. When I struck the match the familiar scent of burning sulphide filled my nostrils like smelling salts, enlivening my senses somewhat. It was light outside; a featureless dishwater rinse of grey sky. I smoked the repellent cigarette as I stared out the window onto a long, narrow yard with half a dozen wilted potted plants and a crumbling old wooden shed at the far end. The cigarette produced shitty brown smoke just how I imagined mustard gas to be. The birds were already well into their raucous morning chatter, so I reckoned it must have been about eight a.m. If things carried on like this I'd end up carted off to the morgue in the back of a meat wagon at the age of only twenty-eight. I was already just a dead body resisting the compulsion to lie down and decompose. I had been born privileged. But I had accepted the privilege like a life sentence. The boredom had become too much. And I had protested by smearing shit all over my own cell walls.

I took a last pull on the cigarette, put the stub in the empty Dr. Pepper can and went through into the next room. Empty beer bottles and all manner of other shit were tossed about on the threadbare carpet. Marvin was propped up in a chair. He was all glammed up like a ponce in a shiny black shirt and silver, pencil-thin tie. He was sitting wrapped in a sleeping

Spiral Out

bag that because of his excessive height only came up to his middle. A burning cigarette hung loosely from his lips. The room was decorated with dismal looking green wallpaper and sections of it were peeling away, exposing patches of damp plaster here and there.

There were two others with Marv who I didn't recognise; a good-looking, young blonde bird whose nipples were in an excited state, showing through a 10,000 Maniacs teeshirt, and a kid with bright copper hair and eyes on the side of his head like a reptile, wearing a great, big, chunky fake gold chain around his neck who must have been her grinning prat of a boyfriend. Fuck knows where they came from. They were kneeling on the floor at the coffee table with gaping mouths, clamouring like starving birds waiting for Mother Marvin to feed them the joint he was rolling. There was an old Bugs Bunny cartoon on the TV inanely blasting away in the corner with nobody watching it. The blonde smiled and the ginger wigger prickface did that flicking the hand thing, snapping two fingers together like the crack of a whip at me and said,

- night wuz wicked man.

- this is Susan and Gavin   Marv pointed with the joint.

I didn't say anything. I felt like punching the reptile kid

in his cunty little face. The little twat with his receding chin was just sitting there like a bag of wet sand not noticing that Marvin was clearly trying to get in his bird's knickers. And like a typical woman she was flirting and lapping it up. I hoped Marv would split her in half with his babseball bat cock, teach her a lesson.

> \- you look like shit Karzoso   Marv observed plaintively running his tongue along the adhesive strip of the cigarette paper   i got some valium if you want some?

I told him I could do with a piss first. I'd already got a system pumped full of speed, ketamine, heroin and booze. I groggily trudged my way up the creaking stairway. A bare light bulb, low wattage, illuminated the dank stairwell in a gloomy yellow haze. In the bathroom I found Six Dogs unconscious, lying on his side on the floor. The filthy bastard had fallen off the toilet with his fucking trousers around his ankles, all pungent shit congealed around his arse. He didn't as much as stir as I stood over him to piss in the toilet. I allowed a little bit of urine to splash on the dirty swine.

On the way home I stopped by the newsagents and bought a carton of milk. At the very least some kind of sustenance to help me regain a bit of strength. But the second a mouthful of the stuff touched my stomach I threw it back up, curdled with yellowy stomach acid.

13

I spent most of the next three days lying sick, sweating, dehydrated in bed. I couldn't even keep a glass of water down. But over the following couple of weeks I slowly recuperated once again, as usual. It was no fucking sweat, been there a dozen times before. My body was still young and regenerative. I'd started to believe myself invincible. I'd imbibed enough drugs and drink to kill a man and I'd now crashed six cars. On one occasion I drank eight pints of beer and sixteen vodkas before putting a Volkswagen Beetle through sixteen foot of Roman wall, down an embankment and landing upside down in a river. And I walked away without a scratch. I literally walked away, leaving the car sunk in the river.

And then there was a knock at the door and fuck me backwards it was Lydia. Still modelling. Still living in London. Up here in Brum for a few days again. Well, I dunno. It musta been twelve months or more. I just flung open the door and gestured for her to come in and straight away she dropped her bag of womanly tricks on the floor and said: well, you look like crap. But after sitting with her for a few moments, for neither

Spiral Out

good nor ill, it felt like she'd never been away and we ended up in bed together. I'd been drifting through life disengaged, people come and people go without much emotional reaction from me. I had to admit Lydia looked as beautiful as ever. She had her make-up all done and her face was as perfect as a little plastic Barbie doll in bright red lipstick and her long black hair tied up in two cute pig-tails. Women are evil; they know precisely how to worm their way right into your bloodstream like a fever. They adapt themselves to exploit a man's weaknesses. For all my invincibility, Lydia rendered me weak to the core.

    The Brigadier was someone I found to be a funny character. Due to infections caused by mainlining Skag he'd had his right arm amputated below the elbow and lost his left leg below the knee. And ever since that he'd taken to hobbling around on a wooden leg with his right sleeve pinned up, wearing a military blazer with a plethora of jangling world war two medals he'd scoured the tat shops for pinned to the left breast. His one eye was also clouded over due to drinking Meths mixed in lime cordial. He apparently riddled out the bitter taste by filtering it through a loaf of bread into a glass. In effect, the bread soaked up the bitter tasting blue colouring they put in the stuff as it drained through. A drink known in some spheres as Blue Train because of this. I always thought some of these people were geniuses in discovering methods to facilitate

Spiral Out

their addictions. I mean some of them should be working on the space program. But if The Brigadier had gone on to live for any greater amount of time he would eventually have ended up completely blind. It's amazing how much hammering the human body can take before it finally gives out. It's only our minds that are made of glass.

  The Brig' survived on a whole swathe of government handouts. Apart from his sick benefit he knew every loophole in the book and claimed for everything he could. And of course he also dealt drugs; he could get his hand(s) on anything. In the pond that he lived in he was, therefore, considered a very wealthy man. He was drippin' in cash, he'd say, proudly. He could afford a drink and a kebab any time he liked.

  I was out of drugs during my few weeks of recuperation and I'd been holed up in my apartment, sweating the sickness out of me without seeing hair nor eye of anyone. Lydia wanted to score so I got on the phone to The Brigadier. He lived on the second floor of an outwardly respectable converted three storey town-house on Lysways Street, about ten miles away in Walsall. He said sure as shit, man, jump in the car and shoot on over and bring the bitch with you.

  - you know Lydia says during the drive over when i take drugs i wonder if this is how good normal people feel all the time and then i realise no no they dont

Spiral Out

cos they aint even got the capacity in the first place.

- come on   I shake my head at her pulling up at the traffic lights in Great Barr and slotting the stick into P you know better than that   they dont think too much thats why they dont need an escape in the first place.

Personality is ephemeral, I remind her. We'd both read the bullshit existentialists. I posit that if she'd been born in 1782 she wouldn't exist as we know her now. We are products of society, socially engineered. Drugs are the only escape. Drugs and... the God delusion, for some. Everything is concrete. For those of us who refuse to accept self-perpetuating delusions: everything is exactly as you see it. There is no greater essence to the rudiments of a rock. A rock is just a rock. The individual alone infuses his own existence with the essence of who he falsely believes himself to be. And Lydia and I had failed to find meaning in our lives because we both saw through all the fucking bullshit. The one thing that we had in common was that we both wanted to die. I hated her beauty, hated it. But I loved her for that reason and I had no doubt that we were in some way fatally connected, like two cells in the same nucleus dying of some disease artificially introduced to the Petri-dish.

Spiral Out

14

- coffees? asks The Brigadier his short bleach-blonde hair all ruffed up.

He's only twenty-seven years old. He's not wearing his wooden leg and is navigating around the clutter of his shit-tip of a place with a walking stick, his trouser leg pinned up and his empty sleeve tucked into the pocket of his jeans. Outside the house looks fine but inside his place is like a derelict house. The TV is sitting on a wooden crate. There's no one else in the building. The occupants on the first and third floors above and below him have moved out and the properties both left vacant. So The Brigadier has broken into the other flats and stolen anything he found left behind.

- here look at this he enthuses.

He's found a Browning 9mm pistol in the upstairs flat. Fuck me! I say, picking it up and turning the cold, dark military green hunk of metal around in my hands, looking at it.

- you got bullets an all?

- yeah look in the clip

Spiral Out

The Brig pokes the air with his finger, a massive grin wiped across his face

- its friggin full man   i always knew there was something dodgy about the cunt who lived up there that gun is a hi power   French military issue   a Browning *Grande Puissance* the Frogs call it.

He takes the gun out my hand and removes the clip. He raises it, squints along the barrel and fires off three imaginary rounds... Click... Click... Click.

The Brigadier's old tin kettle on the gas stove starts whistling in the kitchen. He had his favourite blazer on and the medals clinked together as he hobbles off to make the coffees, leaving Lydia and me sitting on the sofa.

- are we gonna score off this freak or what?   Lydia whispers impatiently.

Yeah, yeah, I assure her, gesturing with my hand for her to simmer down.

- he can turn spiteful   so just go along with him.

Spiral Out

On his walking stick he can't carry the cups so he called me in to help. And the last I remember with any clarity is sitting down to drink the coffee. The Brigadier had every single episode of *The Wacky Races* recorded on VHS tapes and he put one of them on. He had every race on unmarked separate tapes. He used to pick one at random and then take bets on the race winner, a little party game he liked to play. Lydia holds my hand on the sofa. She crashed a round of ciggies and Brig' snatched one, lit it and tossed his lighter on the chair next to him as he reclined to enjoy his smoke.

- dont just throw it down like that   Lydia chastised sitting back and crossing her legs showing off these expensive looking snakeskin cowboy boots   you know *other people here*   so you know   *rude!*

- my house innit bitch   The Brigadier's one good eye scanned her up and down.

- is he always this volatile?

Lydia poked a thumb in his direction.

- pretty much   I laughed.

Spiral Out

- talk about me like im not here The Brigadier sneered you pair of fucking phonies.

Lydia didn't say much else as The Brigadier and I talked a little bit more as we watched the video and bet a few quid just for laughs. Then without warning my hearing and vision seemed to completely dissipate and I felt myself kind of slip sideways down onto the sofa like there was some kind of gyroscopic force fucking with my equilibrium. And the next thing I know I wake up and I am on my own and it's now suddenly it's night and the room was in darkness and my vision was blurred, there was ringing in my ears and a searing pain in my skull. I hadn't been unconscious in the truest sense of the word; I was simply incapacitated, aware of everything around me but in a sickening catatonic trance. I fall off the sofa and rolled onto he floor as if there was a heavy weight on top of me.

So I'm getting up groggily and fumbling about for the light. And I can't explain what happened next. You just sense something is not right. The building was oddly cold and silent. I felt in my gut that something was just wrong and I didn't know what it was. I found the light switch and instinctively picked up The Brig's pistol left on a sideboard that has no doors and looks like he's salvaged it from the rubbish dump and went to inspect the other rooms. My Cuban heeled shoes striking the bare floor boards sounded desolate and harsh.

Across the hall is the bathroom. There is a strange silence and muted glow coming ominously from under the door, so I tentatively toe the door open and go in there. Lydia is in narcosis on the floor; congealed white foam at the corners of her mouth. Brig's military blazer is hanging on the shower rail. He's got her skirt up around her waist, pink knickers around one of her ankles and he's kneeling between her legs, fingering her with his erect cock sticking out his fly-hole.

I leapt across the room and kicked him full in the face sending him crashing backwards into the hand basin. Despite his disability he sprang up shockingly fast on his one leg, grabbing his cut-throat razor off the shelf. He touched his smashed nose and inspected the blood, flicked the blade open and launched himself at me with his bulbous knob still out of his pants screaming:

- im gonna slit your bastard throat!

As he travelled through the air towards me seemingly in slow motion I raised the gun and there was a split-second look of horror on his face before I pulled the trigger and made a Jackson Pollock out of him up the wall. BLAM. Took his head near clean off. What was left of him in the abrupt silence apart from the ringing in my ears went tumbling across the light blue

Spiral Out

tiles like a bag of loose bones. He sagged down in a weird, twisted angle over near the corner of the room, appeared to convulse once and then lay still, dead as a fucking Do-Do. Entry wound on his left cheekbone quite small and neat, heat sealed clean. The back of his skull all but blown apart.

I got hold of Lydia and began rubbing my knuckles briskly over her breast-bone and giving her mouth to mouth. I repeated the procedure over and over until after what seemed like ages she came round, choking and spitting and moaning. I sat her up gently and leaned her head into the bath tub, stuck my fingers down her throat and induced vomiting. I'd barely ever seen the size 8 girl eat, she was puking nothing but watery, green stomach bile streaked with yellow.

- its okay   I told her serenely as she coughed and spat a last mouthful of vomit into the bath   its all okay.

15

So I'm in this phone box on the corner outside the *Dog and Partridge* pub waiting agitatedly when Offenbach dutifully rings back from his DynaTac and I explain best I can what just happened. Messy, he says, calmly. Very messy.

Spiral Out

    - just leave the body there   he advises   its not like anyone of note is going to give a fuck about him   could be months before anyone raises the alarm.

There's not much option in such an unplanned situation, Offenbach says. A clean-up job in this situation could carry more risk than it's worth. Stay calm, just go home and burn every fibre of clothing Lydia and I were both wearing and scrub yourselves clean with an anti-bacterial wash. There was no way the gun could be traced to me so don't sweat it, I was to just wipe it clean and chuck it down next to the body and get the fuck out of there. Walk away calmly, as if nothing is wrong, don't bring attention to ourselves.

    He asked if I parked the black Merc outside the flat. I told him no, there weren't any spaces so I parked it around the corner on the main road. People are not very observant anyway, Offenbach said, approximately twenty-five percent of people in prison have been erroneously identified by so called witnesses. And there's countless more felons walking amongst us because none of the dozy fuckers ever see anything with any degree of accuracy. But that car would potentially have stuck out like a sore thumb. No one making note of the car in the vicinity was one less thing to worry about. The best thing the pair of you can do is get out of there and act as if nothing has happened. There's dozens of these unsolved killings every week. Lock up

Spiral Out

the doors, Offenbach instructed, and then take the keys and throw them in a canal miles away. But do it quickly. The longer the body lay there degenerating the harder their job would be.

Not many people had heard of Rohypnol in the late eighties. It had been in use in America since the seventies and at that time it had just come to our shores but was widely unknown until later in the 90's. It was only years later I realised that that must have been the stuff The Brigadier had most likely spiked our coffees with.

I kept checking the papers and the TV for a while, for months afterwards in fact. For a while it haunted me quite a bit. I thought about the traffic passing obliviously by The Brigadier's flat. And him lying there unaware of the sound of it. Days and nights revolving around his passive, decaying remains. Amazing really but I never heard anything about him again in the papers and I eventually stopped thinking about the whole she-bang. At times I even wondered whether I'd imagined the whole thing in some drugged-up reverie. If he'd been a normal, tax-paying member of society they'd probably have left no stone unturned but the authorities really must have come along and scraped him up off the floor like a piece of dogshit and that was that.

I heard people around town, in the bars, say things like oh fuck The Brigadier's dead and people talked about how it was suspicious because apparently the flat was locked from the

Spiral Out

outside, so something must have leaked out on the grapevine somehow -- but there was not a sausage from the authorities or the media. Nobody gave a fuck though; it was all just gossip, something to talk about amidst their empty lives. But for all I know they'd swiftly arrested the former tenant from upstairs who'd left the gun behind and thought they'd wrapped it all up with a nice bow. That's a theory that made most sense to me.

16

Lydia stayed with me for a few days, both of us recovering from it all, the effects of the Rohypnol wore off relatively quickly over most of the next day and after that there were no lasting effects at all. And then Lydia packed her stuff and headed off for a London modelling assignment again as if none of it had happened. The door closed behind her once more, leaving those familiar waves of emptiness, a lipstick stain on a wine glass to remind me that she'd even been there.

The sun came up over the tower blocks and another day began. I was awoken by tiny stones being thrown up at my bedroom window. I got out of bed and went over and looked down on the street. It was five in the morning and Six Dogs was down there standing in the piss-stain I'd left the night before, dragging a black dustbin liner along the street with him

Spiral Out

and puffing on a big Cuban. As usual he had his blue Kagool on. But he was also wearing his beat-up party hat, looking like the Mad Hatter.

    - let me the fuck up quick   he waved his arms anxiously   ive done Edgbaston Cricket Club over.

I buzzed him up and a few seconds later he dashed through the door dragging this clinking bag and saying he thought the police might have followed him. Jesus H. Christ I yelled, don't get bringing them round here with you, for fuck sake. Yeah, he'd broken into the cricket club pavilion, fuckin piss-easy, he chimed, and raided their bar and then shot straight up here on the bus with his swag.

    He reached into the bag and handed me a bottle of *Glenfidich,* telling me to calm the fuck down with a smile on his lips. Relax, Six Dogs grins and shakes his head cheerily, the rozzers saw him get off the bus but he's pretty sure he lost them when he darted under Paradise Circus subway. This boddle's for you, and take whatever else you want, he beamed. So I shrug and get some glasses from the kitchen. Six Dogs slipped out of his Kagool and we sat down and cracked open a few drinks. Six Dogs was even filthier than usual, he looked like he'd washed his face in Castrol GTX. By eight-o-clock that morning I was shit-faced on a cocktail of whisky and vodka again. We carried on drinking, disposing of the evidence, all day and through until evening when we walked the short distance from my flat to *Snobs* nightclub.

We met up with Marvin in there who was leaning at the bar trying to chat up some bird with blue hair by telling her about the size of his cock. Six Dogs has crashed the Cubans because he says that's what you do when you have a slice of fortune -- you share it with your friends -- and Marv's gripping one between his thumb and forefinger, leaning back from this bird with an overtly casual air and I overhear him going: yeah, yeah, you know whatta mean?

> - its as if God came down from heaven   he asserts   touched me on the crotch and said my gift to you my son   now go forth amongst the women of your land and give them pleasure.

The blue haired girl doesn't look impressed and Marv watches her pick up her drinks with a sarcastic smile and wander off, disappearing into the heaving mass on the dance floor jumping up and down in unison to the thwacking bass line of the Stooges *I Got A Right*. Marv shrugs and slides his elbow along the bar to the next one, blowing cigar smoke pseudo-suavely in the air:

Spiral Out

> - before youre thirty im gonna have fucked *you* of course it takes a special kind of woman who can you know cater for some of my very special sexual requirements.

He'll carry on like this all night until he finds some poor cow who succumbs. Marv will succeed somewhere in the end, he always does. The second girl walks off shaking her head, too. But he remains undeterred and later on, sure as shit, as predicted he looks to be making headway with some skank over by the food bar. I am slumped down on my own, shit-faced at a table in the corner near the strange bubble wall they had down there that trips you out in the disco lights. Marv comes sauntering over, flashing me the A-OK sign with his hand. He leaned into me and said covertly out the corner of his mouth,

> - making progress with this one Karzy wuz beginning to think wed fuckin come on lesbian night.

Six Dogs doesn't even enter the equation of success, lesbian night or not. He clumsily crashed against the bar and tottered about precariously on the balls of his feet, telling some eighteen year old light-skinned black girl she looks like Mike Tyson. In a minute he'll have his own cock out, waggling it at

Spiral Out

her and going:

    - watch out love its anny a little un but its a fuckin mad bastard!

I staggered home on my own, completely out of my tree. All my clothes were dishevelled and booze-soaked. I grabbed the telephone and belled Lydia to ask her if she wanted to run away to France with me. She wanted to know what the fuck I was playing at ringing her at this hour. I'm serious, I slurred down the phone:

    - run away to France with me.

Mark, the fucking bitch replies, getting all up on her high-horse again, talking with that tone I've heard a dozen times before like I'm some kind of cockroach; I have a boyfriend down here who I am in love with. I suppose I should have told you before we slept together. But she made a mistake, she stresses with a moan. A mistake (again) for Christ's sake? And then she starts asking me as a friend to forget about it. I slammed the phone down on her. For fuck sake, what did she mean, asking me as a friend? I'll never comprehend the fucking bitches. Never. I can understand perfectly why they used to burn the evil fucking bitches at the

Spiral Out

stake. Well, if she thought I was banking on her she was mistaken. I would be going regardless.

I took the framed Polaroid of Lydia from my writing desk. It was the one she sent me from Terracina, by a restaurant overlooking the sea and she's wearing a short blue and white polka-dot summer dress. I realised it was the only picture of her I had; and in fact, the only vestige of her being I would ever truly possess. I remembered Lydia coming around one time and saying,

> - one thing ive noticed about you you have absolutely no photographs of your family anywhere   thats very strange, you know?   why dont you have any photographs?

I looked at her and said truthfully,

- i dont know.

I slid Lydia's photo out of the frame and screwed it up, went into the kitchen, placed it in the sink and set fire to it with my lighter. The pungent smoke produced as her image shrivelled away into nothing was just as formless as all the hopes and dreams I had at one time foolishly built around her. I'd romanticised the whole foundation of the relationship.

There had been no love involved. It had been a self-inflicted hallucination; something I'd desperately wanted to believe in. When I thought about it all now she had never really reciprocated my affection. That's why I didn't keep photographs – because both dreams and memories are painful and meaningless. They don't mean anything, filtered through the mesh of our own desires and hopes and needs as opposed to grounded in reality. I swilled the burnt ashes down the plughole.

In the bedroom, where Lydia's presence even now seemed to hang in the air like a ghost, I had my two suitcases packed. I'd secretly been thinking for some time now about where I could go. I'd arranged to put the Merc into dry storage and intended on fucking off to the south of France and simply loafing around in the sunshine for a while, smoking cigarettes, drinking all their wine. After that I could carry on to Spain, or anywhere, just keep on moving. No one would be able to find me.

17

I had been numb for I don't know how many weeks. No feelings left for anyone and anything. Just a dead-eyed stare greeting me every morning in the bathroom mirror. I felt

Spiral Out

nothing stirring inside me; if I'd taken a kitchen knife and sliced open my arm I was sure the wound wouldn't even have bled. In the mirror my eyes were like two dull stones. Every day became the same, each frozen hour slowly seeping through my bones like mescaline, until finally, at that moment, the ticking clock on the motel room wall stopped dead and the stark discharge of silence roused me from a state of catatonia.

The dead heart corrodes. Like a ship at the bottom of an ocean. Grey drum of neglected memories in silent abyss, where fish turn and twist, flickering like silver coins in its steel carcass of lost souls. You stick that wire in your veins and it numbs you just a little bit more with each and every fix. Whatever morsel of humanity was born within me did not live very long.

Five o'clock in the morning. I was probably the only guest in the place awake, lying there bombed out of my brain, minute twitches in the muscles in my arms and legs. I rolled off the bed and indolently started packing my suitcase.

I'd been drifting between petrol stations and motels, trying to run away from it all. Beneath skies peppered with stars white as boneskulls, so pin-eyed the motorway lights burned my retinas like napalm. I didn't like who I'd been most of my life, all I wanted was to spend my days in a state of intoxication; to create around me a kind if sensory deprivation chamber, a flotation tank of sorts.

Spiral Out

As I fired up the engine and sat waiting for the blowers to defrost the windscreen the thought occurred to me: I could stay here. I watched a ship heading towards the horizon. I wanted to be on the fucker, diminishing into nothing. Don't even recall where the place was, somewhere in Scotland, tried to get as far away as I could. Something was drawing me back, it seemed. I don't remember properly, it's all a fog in my mind. But that's what happens. Drink and drugs anaesthetise you. You end up drifting emptily through your days without feeling pain any more. That's why you start taking drugs in the first place. And eventually you become so numb you don't care who you hurt in return. In a sense drugs normalise you. Every hit further hardens you against the elements until your outer shell is nothing but unfeeling scar tissue. Drugs make uniquely sensitive people as numb and oblivious and uncaring as everyone else in the world. But essentially, when it comes right down to it, we're all of us alike; we are all just a feather at the mercy of a hurricane.

But I could stay here... Spend my hollow days throwing pebbles in the sea. Summer nights lying on the beach shooting imaginary bullets at the stars. I fantasised about living in a lighthouse where I could watch the sea alone, letting memories peel away from me like dead skin cells. In a universe where even the oceans are ultimately ephemeral I could drown in cold isolation and no one would ever substantiate my having ever

Spiral Out

existed at all.

One by one the stars had vanished and the early morning sky became a wash of white nothingness now. Just bleached, white plainness as far as the eye could see. There wasn't a soul visible on the icy streets. I put the Spacemen 3 on the stereo, shoved it into D and lurched away into the void.

The motorway unfurled endlessly before me; stretching all the way back to the concrete oblivion of where I came from. I supposed I was returning through some residue of hope left inside me. I shifted along in a trance, uniformly beneath the featureless white clouds in the lines of traffic like I was on a conveyor belt.

About halfway home I stopped at a service station and had a coffee and a jam doughnut. Outside on the car park I noticed a scabby-headed woman in plastic flip-flops with clumps of hair falling out and patchy, flaking skin, pregnant to the hilt, smoking a cigarette. She already had one toddler, still in nappies, running about. The kid started playing in a dirty puddle. She grabbed hold of him by the scruff of the neck and yanked him away yelling:

- touch that again and im gonna rip your arms right out their sockets you little cunt!

I mean Christ on the crapper, who would have gone and

fucked a woman like that? She was an emblem of everything that disgusted me about humanity, not even caring about the new life budding inside her. Certainly, modern government is a dirty job; having to go around doing nothing but wiping the shitty backsides of its useless populace. Nepotism gives birth to a new generation of scum. But what the fuck? The human race is on a random collision course with its collective destiny, with no distinction between the beautiful and the damned.

18

Not as it matters. We live in a frightening world where all the safety nets are illusions anyway. Like an animal born deficient in some way; the rest of the pack reject it and kill it. In much the same way, the human race terminates the deformed, whether it's mentally or physically. When you think about it death itself is but a moment in time. It passes just as anything else passes.

This is a physical universe; brutal and unforgiving, and barring terminal illness or suicide you're condemned to endure it for decades. Objectively I know the world can at times be a beautiful place. I can appreciate the sunrise glinting momentarily off a frosted window pane. I comprehend the symbolism of a single blade of grass, alone amongst so many other blades of grass. But death is the end and these white-light near death experiences are proof of nothing. It's just a life of indoctrination reaching a single point of infinity.

As the next day began to kick in one by one the usual crowd formed on the street. The same amorphous mass as any other day, all frantically going about their routines. Even the beautiful ones seem to me nothing more than an assembly of biological substances. Of course, matters have improved drastically. In the middle-ages only the educated elite could read and write. These days the average member of the proletariat can both read, write *and* understand basic economics better than apes by a wide margin.

I can feel something crawling over the whole city, an overbearing sense of contagion permeating every dark, piss-stained alley like The Black Death. The fact that I spit blood stark against the white porcelain basin merely confirms that I still have some blood inside me. But it doesn't feel like blood any more than oil pumping through the steel cylinders of an inanimate machine.

I'd been searching for a feeling or some way to feel something but I always end up just sitting staring listlessly from the window thinking about how the bones of the dead are down there beneath our feet somewhere.

All those revolutions of the past have failed. There is neither virtue nor purpose in fighting for what you believe in.

Spiral Out

That's all been debunked time and time again. Dictatorial governments keep redefining and re-establishing themselves no matter what. Fuck the world off. Nihilism is the only revolt left. Don't vote. Don't not vote. Complete inaction is our only action. Dead men pay no taxes. Hard drugs are my generation's revolution. And the generation after that, and the one after that. Tune out. Turn off. Kill yourself.

All passion within me died a long time ago. With every passing day I find it more difficult to look upon the horror that is the human face. I only see the masks people wear. I see only the masks and the counterfeit mechanical movements of their facial muscles. And it is a terrifying thought; that we are all cold and alone and everything around us is soulless, made of stone and steel and blood and soil. And what makes it so terrifying is that I know what I perceive is not just the reality of everything but also the machinations of my own fractured mind.

Hours later and I was in the 350SL, white as a ghost and sweating, going for a night-drive with the roof down. Amped out of my skull, rolling down the Aston Expressway. The jet black '79 SL was ten years old now, still worth a pretty penny or two; it'd been an eighteenth birthday present from my parents. I was wearing my vintage leather biker jacket that I bought from *The Razor's Edge* on Hurst Street in 1987. I'd read Albert Camus's *The Rebel* and various philosophies of

Spiral Out

Nietzsche and of course I accepted there were deeper philosophical explorations to be argued about the nature of rebellion. But I looked at in more simple terms: all a man needs is a black leather jacket with a pocketful of Gonzales. It was more in symbols than in deeds. And on that score I was more in tune with Carl Jung's theories.

Ahead of me the monochrome blast of white city lights strung out like diamonds, a swirling mass glittering on the apex of amphetamine charged night. I was down to skin and bone. I hadn't eaten anything in two days and my nerves were stripped down to the bare wire. I caught my reflection in the door mirror and laughed. One hundred-and-ten miles an hour, my face fixed in a taut, cadaverous grimace, mad at the wheel. If the police pulled me over now I'd tell them Einstein's theory of relativity was wrong and that current laws of physics could not put a cap on maximum achievable speed. Every cell in my body reverberated to the murderously heavy bass line of The Jesus and Mary Chain's *Sidewalking* and the dazzling kaleidoscope of headlights trailing in my rear view mirror. I'm winging it through the glittering city again and right at this point in time it feels like I aint never gonna come down and this brilliant night will last forever. I don't even know where I'm heading but I'm absolutely bombed, gripping the wheel and thinking *here I come... Here I come!*

I swing it round by the law courts and when I get stuck

at a red light at the pedestrian crossing some bird clattering down the street on heels shouts:

- nice car fella!

To which her friend with a beer-gut and legs that are too chunky for the short leopard print skirt she's wearing replies as loudly as she can,

- yeah   pity about the dickhead driving it   ha ha ha ha!

Well, she doesn't exactly look a million Liras herself to me. I wait until the light turns green because the last thing I want is to give this bitch the satisfaction of being able to kick the car - and when the light flips I look at her and yell:

- says you   you fat cunt!   before cackling with derisive laughter and pulling away with the V8 rumbling under the bonnet.

19

When I see old black and white newsreel footage I see streets swarming with people from another time. Whole

Spiral Out

generations who are now dead. They lived and loved but their meaningless lives are now lost in the morass of obscurity. It all strikes me as so futile. One day I and everyone around me will also be just another extinct generation, forgotten bone-ash beneath future foundations. And despite all this there is a certain element of sadness I feel. I feel sadness because at the same time I know man is delicate and cannot last in the same way that a flower cannot last. There is an elusive beauty to us, no matter how profoundly difficult it is to quantify.

There's nothing to worry about any more. In the end everything is silent and beautiful. Just a pull of the trigger and in one split second, spread your bloody brains across the ceiling. Blam! The only thing left is for some poor bastard to come and scrape your oblivious, blood soaked carcass up off the floor. It's the end of a cycle of life that couldn't have had any other possible outcome. All it takes is one split second. Flip the kill-switch. Press the button. Whatever. On television and in magazines it's all perpetual friendship and smiles, iced cocktails and golden, palm-treed beaches. I just want to shut myself away in a fortress of my own making. I want to erect impenetrable walls around myself.

There will be no suicide note. It wouldn't achieve anything. Who would even read it with any true understanding of who I am? But I will cut off a flower. A beautiful, blood-red Dahlia. And hold it in the withered hands I was born with, a final offering of love to a world that never loved me back. There is no laughter down here. We are each born into pain. Right from the moment your mother's pelvic bone cracks, That bastard God alone sits up there sucking on blood-oranges and spitting out the pips with sardonic laughter.

- Ha Ha Ha Ha.

I am condemned to this metaphysical nightmare of being able to look into the iniquities of the human soul. And yet I breath the air with unfeeling iron lungs.

20

Unable to sleep again I stood unleashing a bright green stream of piss out the window onto the street. I was waiting for the last stupendous holocaust to just blow everything in sight away; to flatten this whole city. But nothing ever changes. Staring at the sky, those myriad stars I'd so many times sat and counted with dilated eyes, wanting to shoot them outta the sky while speeding out my head, obstinately remained. In the kitchen cupboards I had only a bag of potatoes, a bunch of bananas and some pickled onions and all I could think about was whether it'd be possible to cook something up from this

Spiral Out

meagre ingredients that I could extract some kind of mind-altering substance from. Through the wall I could just about hear the muffled sound of the neighbour's television transmitting its usual stream of bland information at three-o-clock in a lost and fragmented morning.

I stood at the basin splashing cold water on my face in the public toilets at New Street Station, where in the bright strip-lighting I caught the mirror image of myself. It stopped me in my tracks. At first I didn't exactly recognise it as me. It was a colder looking image than I would have expected. A pale unfeeling face with unmoving graphite eyes that peered back at me, asking: when was the last time that man felt a human emotion? I was disconnected from the world. From myself. I was a construct. Pale skin of hardened plaster. I could almost hear the machine-like vrrrrrrrr as my pupils automatically adjusted to the light.

On the tiled floor, wet with piss, there was a discarded torn out page from a porno magazine. A pair of spread thighs, softly haired blonde cunt filled the frame. I finished my piss and walked back out onto the deserted platform, kicking a squashed Coke can down onto the tracks. I checked I'd got my ticket in my pocket. The first train for the 200 mile trip to Dover where I was to jump on the ferry to France as a foot passenger was due at 5.10 am. I ambled idly to the far end of the platform where I could see the red digital clock on the top of the Rotunda glowing against the muted early morning sky. 5.16. The train was typically late with no announcements over the Tannoy.

My physical responses were supplanting all ability to feel. It is a clinical rejection of emotional warmth, acquiesced to the pursuit of only physical gratification; an animalisation where intellectualism, too, had been rejected. I wasn't interested in the biological evolution or chemical composition of the orange: I was interested only in digesting its sweet juices, intent on sustaining my own existence in the cocoon of numbness I was trying to insulate myself with.

In effect, I was not only running from pain, but from the very notion of pain. My world was losing polarity and I was compelled to seek greater and greater release. It set the precept for the rest of my life. I was to desire everything to carnal excess in an effort to avoid emotional conflict. In the end, without even realising it, I had indeed grown a hardened shell around me. The emotional traits that I had so insensibly stripped humans of I had instead begun to project onto my possessions. I wondered whether this was born out of my natural inclination towards control. I knew I couldn't control the natural element of electricity that flows between two people. But I could control my own connection with inanimate objects. I craved them. I scoured antique shops, wanting to surround myself with items of aesthetic beauty.

Many years ago I'd chanced upon a heavy old hunk of a Russian camera in a junk shop. I imagined what scenes it might once have captured during Russian industrialisation; monstrous structures of steel chemical plants belching clouds of thick black smoke over those freezing Russian cityscapes. The machine had more soul than any person I had ever met. And as it sat on my sideboard; nothing more than an aesthetic piece of black and chrome memorabilia, I felt that it craved the touch of fingertips on its shutter-release button so that sad dead eye could blink into life again.

Staring at the tracks extending into grey dilapidated vicinities of steel girders, granite and glass in either direction it struck me that the birds perched disinterested along the power cables looked like they knew something I didn't. The sky was aptly just a featureless dirty white death shroud, no face of Christ etched into the linen. No image of the Virgin Mary in the cold, soggy piece of toast they'd fobbed me off with at the café. The British Rail Intercity 125 finally approached, clattering its way around the bend on the approach to the platform. It started to rain just as it rolled into the station and I dunno whether it was a morsel of hope or what but as I climbed aboard I had a strange feeling the grey clouds might well clear up later and it'd turn out to be a sunny day.

As the train pulled out of the station I sat spooning

peach halves in sweet syrup into my mouth straight from the tin. The only other entities in the carriage were a mother with a tiny baby. It all slips away from us so quickly, I thought, I'd be an old man by the time that child is forty years old.

It's all transitory and futile. In the end we're all so fucking insignificant. Even the hand that writes these words will one day be dust. I will be gone from this world, vanquished. And there will be whole future generations I will never know; a completely different landscape I'll know nothing of. It is to those future generations I offer my love across the cruel boundaries of time. These words are the only treasure of me having ever existed at all, I hope in some way they hold up. I am a man out of time and out of place. To the future I express my sorrow that we will never meet, yours will perhaps be a better world, and one that I could perhaps have found comfort in. On the side of the tin of peaches it read: net weight - 14 Oz.

The End.

PHOTO BY u.v. ray

u.v.ray is an internationally published writer. His work has been skirting the fringes of the underground literary scene for a period spanning three decades.

He dropped out of school at the age of fifteen without any academic qualifications, spending the next twenty-five years drifting around bars and nightclubs across the U.K, Europe and the United States. It's almost certainly for the better that most of his writing during this time has been lost forever.

His second chapbook *Road Trip & Other Poems* was published by Erbacce Press in 2011. A collection of short stories *We Are Glass* and the long-awaited novella *Spiral Out* were published by Murder Slim Press in 2013.

WE ARE GLASS by u.v. ray

"u.v. ray is by turns passionate, angered, insightful and rebellious... Great writing removes the lid from the rotting can, it challenges the false and empty symbol. u.v. ray does that with aplomb."
---Richard Godwin (author of *Mr. Glamour*), Introduction to *We Are Glass*

"u.v. ray's *We Are Glass* is a must have. Buy it, consume it, and ask for seconds. I did."
---Adam Campbell, *9Sense Podcast*

Trade paperback size
167 pages

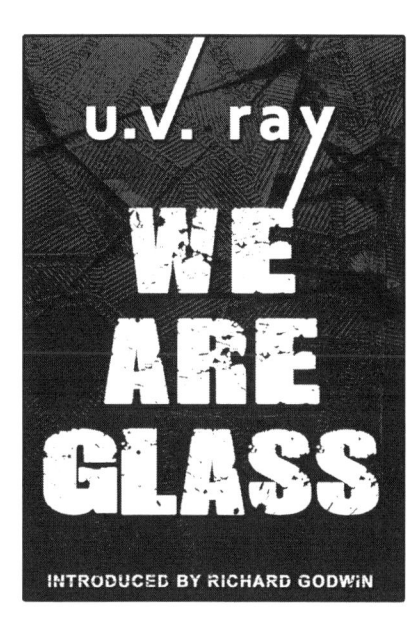

WHY ME by Seymour Shubin

"*Why Me?* communicates complex ideas with simplicity, honesty and skill. And, as a result, it's yet another form of writing that Seymour Shubin has mastered. What the hell will he do next?"
---Steve Hussy (author of *Steps*), Introduction to *Why Me?*

40 poems
The first truly autobiographical work by legendary author Seymour Shubin (*Anyone's My Name, The Hunch*)

Chapbook size
78 pages

MURDER SLIM PRESS
www.murderslim.com

STEPS by Steve Hussy

"*Steps* knocked me sideways the first time I read it, and further reads diminished none of its power. To read *Steps* is to see the absurdities at the heart of all relationships revealed under the spotlight's glare."
--- Tony O'Neill, Introduction to *Steps*

"Hussy treads the same broken path [as] Bukowski and Fante... Yet he has a distinct poetic voice, a voice made his own. And the music? A harrowing Waitsian blues."
--- Susan Tomaselli, *Dogmatika*

Chapbook size
62 pages

LONELY NO MORE by Seymour Shubin

"Seymour Shubin knows his way around the short story because of the deceptive ease of his prose. But as you're swept into the momentum of any given tale it's easy to overlook all of his other considerable strengths: he's incredibly perceptive, touching, funny, compassionate and versatile, among a host of other qualities."
--- Mark SaFranko, from the Introduction to *Lonely No More*

Sixteen crime and confessional stories
Cover Art by Richard Watts. Lavish interior art
Trade paperback size
128 pages

MURDER SLIM PRESS
www.murderslim.com

THE HUNCH by **Seymour Shubin**

"Seymour fills his books with genuine emotion and small human touches... as well as keen psychological insights. *The Hunch* is... gripping and haunting [because] the anguish and trauma that this couple go through are genuine and heartfelt."
---Dave Zeltserman (author of *Pariah*), Introduction to *The Hunch*

"Seymour Shubin is a great crime author... [and] the novel is a delight to read."
---Rod Loft, *Bookgasm*

Trade paperback size
184 pages

LONERS by **Mark SaFranko**

"Mark SaFranko dazzles with *Loners*, an addictive, wide-ranging collection of crime stories of the highest order, and some of the most compelling character-driven fiction I've read in years. Very highly recommended."
--- Jason Starr (author of *Cold Caller*)

Introduced by **Seymour Shubin** - author of *Lonely No More* and *The Hunch*
Eight pages of interior art by **Richard Watts** and **Steve Hussy**

Trade paperback size
216 pages

MURDER SLIM PRESS
www.murderslim.com

HATING OLIVIA by Mark SaFranko

"The words 'raw,' 'brutal,' 'addictive' and 'brilliant' are so overused they have almost lost their meaning, but they are fitting descriptions of a memoir from a very, very talented author."
--- James Doorne, *Bizarre Magazine*

"If you're a Miller or Bukowski fan then *Hating Olivia* is fresh meat, a gift tied together with a blood-stained bow."
--- Dan Fante (author of *Mooch, Chump Change*), Introduction to *Hating Olivia*

Trade paperback size
220 pages

LOUNGE LIZARD by Mark SaFranko

"With the publication of *Lounge Lizard* a ground-breaking moment has occurred... I envy the fact that you still have the jolting, pulsating, eye-opening experience of reading *Lounge Lizard* ahead of you."
--- Joseph Ridgwell, *Bookmunch*

"Here comes *Lounge Lizard*, a novel written by one hardnosed, kick-ass, American original."
--- Dan Fante (author of *Mooch, Chump Change*), Introduction to *Lounge Lizard*

Trade paperback size
216 pages

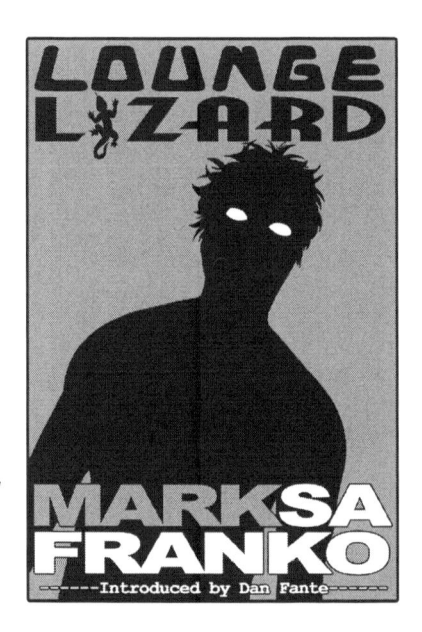

MURDER SLIM PRESS
www.murderslim.com

GOD BLESS AMERICA by Mark SaFranko

"*God Bless America* is strong stuff. Vomit, blood, piss. Guts. All delivered in scathing, acid prose. SaFranko does not spare the reader in this brutal powerhouse of a novel."
--- Mary Dearborn (author of *The Happiest Man Alive: A Biography of Henry Miller*), Introduction to *God Bless America*

"[It] is not only a passionate character study, it is also beautiful dirty realist fiction in the grand American tradition."
--- Matthew Firth, *Front and Centre*

Trade paperback size
278 pages

THE ANGEL by Tommy Trantino

"Tommy Trantino has given us the works - from A to TZZIT. He has put it all in one book replete with maniacal illustrations as a handbook to Eternity."
--- Henry Miller

"I haven't read a book in a long time that has hit me so hard -- a book so fierce, so poetic, so wise, so heartbreaking."
--- Howard Zinn

In print for the first time in 30 years
Introduced by Tony O'Neill
Chapbook size
92 pages

MURDER SLIM PRESS
www.murderslim.com

NAM by Robert McGowan

"[*NAM* approaches its] troubling subject from all sides, chipping away at the mysterious monolith that was the American war [and] Robert McGowan displays remarkable range and depth."
---Stewart O'Nan, editor of *The Vietnam Reader*, a Vietnam War based anthology

"[A] dazzling, harsh, funny and truthful book."
---*The Veteran*

8 Pages of Interior Art by Steve Hussy
Trade paperback size
218 pages

A LONG PERAMBULATION
by **Robert McGowan**

"I was deeply moved. It is a brilliant meditation on life and death. Elegantly written and utterly original, this book will surely endure."
--- Robert Olen Butler,
Pulitzer Prize-Winning Author of
A Good Scent From A Strange Mountain

"Heartfelt and utterly beautiful, yet grounded in strength, integrity, and conviction. McGowan at his very best."
--- Christine Cote, Founder, Shanti Arts.

Trade paperback size
68 pages

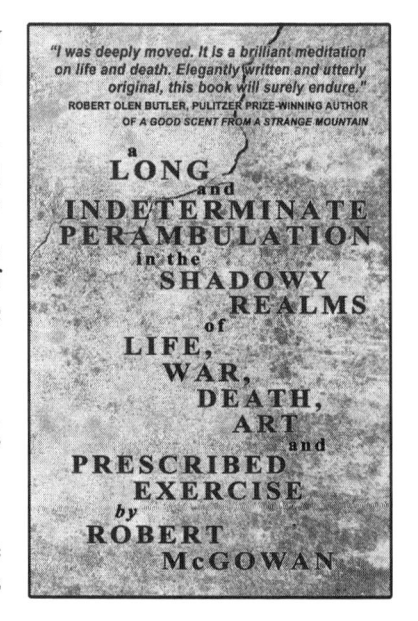

MURDER SLIM PRESS
www.murderslim.com

THE SAVAGE KICK #5
featuring:
Ivan Brunetti: Interview & **Cartoons** / *Another Tough Time* by **Mark SaFranko** / *Deadly Spanking* by **Jim Hanley** / *First* by **Steve Hussy** / *Slut, Bitch, Whore* by **Julie Kazimer** / **Seymour Shubin**: Interview & *Lonely No More* / *Worse Feeling There Is* by **Robert McGowan** / *Bloody Virtue* by **Jeffrey Bacon** / *Carl of Hollyweird* by **Kevin O'Kendley** / *Halloween* by **J.R. Helton** / **Joe R. Lansdale**: Interview & *One Of Them* / *SK's Picks of 2009* / Cover by **Richard Watts** / 10 Pages of Art by **Steve Hussy**

Triple sized / 232 pages

THE SAVAGE KICK #6
featuring:
Dan Fante: Interview & **Point Doom** excerpt
Dead To Rights by **Seymour Shubin**
The First Flower by **u.v. ray**
Slug by **Steve Hussy**
Debbie Drechsler: Interview & *Daddy Knows Best* / *The Target* by **Kevin O'Kendley**
Headache by **William Hart**
Innocent by **Aaron Garrison**
Prison Prose by **Jeffrey Frye**
Morning by **Matthew Wilding**
Things That Weren't True by **Rob McGowan**
Savage Kick's Picks of 2010 and 2011
Cover & 12 Pages of Art by **Steve Hussy**

Triple sized / 206 pages

MURDER SLIM PRESS
www.murderslim.com

MURDERSLIM.COM
Welcome to the wrong side of the tracks

Find us on: facebook

FOLLOW US ON twitter

@MurderSlimPress

MURDER SLIM PRESS
www.murderslim.com

Printed in Great Britain
by Amazon.co.uk, Ltd.,
Marston Gate.